THE LAST BRIDGE

THE LAST BRIDGE

Ann Redmayne

Chivers
Bath, England

•

Thorndike Press
Waterville, Maine USA

This Large Print edition is published by BBC Audiobooks Ltd, England, and by Thorndike Press, USA.

Published in 2003 in the U.K. by arrangement with the author.

Published in 2003 in the U.S. by arrangement with Juliet Burton Literary Agency.

U.K. Hardcover ISBN 0–7540–7252–5 (Chivers Large Print)
U.K. Softcover   ISBN 0–7540–7253–3 (Camden Large Print)
U.S. Softcover   ISBN 0–7862–5407–6 (Nightingale Series)

The text of this Large Print edition is unabridged.
Other aspects of the book may vary from the original edition.

Set in 16 pt. New Times Roman.

Printed in Great Britain on acid-free paper.

British Library Cataloguing in Publication Data available

Library of Congress Cataloging-in-Publication Data

Redmayne, Ann.
  The last bridge / Ann Redmayne.
      p.   cm.
  ISBN 0–7862–5407–6 (lg. print : sc : alk. paper)
  1. Large type books. I. Title.
PR6118.E45L38 2003
823'.92—dc21   2003047378

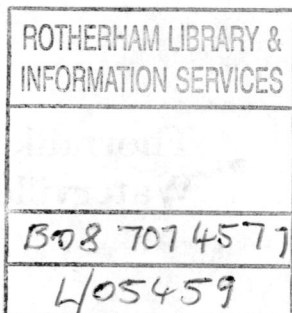

CHAPTER ONE

'Frances, you must come at once!' Fran heard
her grandmother on the phone and hearing
her use her full name, Frances, Fran Marchant
knew instantly there was something wrong.

'Gran, what is it? Are you ill? Has
something happened to the house?'

'It's the silliest thing. I've fallen and broken
my leg.'

'Where are you? When did it happen?'

'Now just take a deep breath and calm
down,' Elizabeth Marchant ordered firmly.

Doing as she was told, Fran smiled wryly. It
was typical of Gran to tell her to calm down.
She and Fran were exact opposites. Gran took
things very much as they came; Fran tended to
cross bridges before she came to them.

'It's not often I can thank my lucky stars
that an out-of-character action of yours works
out for the best. But you walking out of that
advertising agency last week means you can
come up here and look after things.'

'Are you still at The Court?' Fran asked,
raking her long, fair hair away from her face.

'Of course not! I'm in hospital but
tomorrow I'm going to a nursing home until
this wretched plaster is off.'

'Why don't you go back to The Court?' Fran
asked anxiously, wondering if the fracture

1

wasn't as straightforward as Elizabeth was making out. 'Mrs Bowen and I could look after you.'

Elizabeth didn't reply at once, but when she did, she sounded weary.

'Fran, now I don't want you worrying, but the doctors think I need a complete rest. It seems they think that at my age, I bit off more than I could chew getting The Court ready for opening to the public. But enough about me! Will you go to The Court to look after things?'

'Of course I will! But I wish you had told me earlier that getting the house ready for the opening was making you ill.'

'I am not ill!' Elizabeth said firmly. 'All you have to do is check that everyone is doing their job properly.'

'But I haven't the slightest idea who is supposed to be doing what!'

'If you had been up to see what was happening, instead of chasing after that good-for-nothing boyfriend . . .'

Elizabeth knew she had touched Fran's raw nerve, but she hadn't the time or energy to be tactful. The last thing Fran needed was to be reminded of Geoff, so Fran hurriedly interrupted her grandmother.

'I expect I'll manage, and anyway it will do me good to be away from Bristol for a while.'

'Thank you, that's a load off my mind. Now I can concentrate on getting better. Ring me if you hit any problems. I'll let you know the phone number of the nursing home when I get there. But I must stop now. That torturer of a physiotherapist is marching towards me.'

It was early that evening when Fran drove west across the Severn Bridge into Monmouthshire, the window of the car down as though the wind would blow away every memory of Geoff. In her rear mirror she saw mountainous black clouds over Bristol. She hoped this was symbolic, leaving behind the darkness which had enveloped her since she had discovered Geoff in an amorous embrace with his secretary.

It seemed everyone at the agency had known of his affair with Anita, everyone, that is, except Fran. Even now as she took the road north from the bridge, Fran's mouth hardened into a straight line. She had walked out of his office, head held high and that was the last she'd seen of him.

The tourist season hadn't started so the roads were quiet and it did not take her long to reach The Court, nestling in a deep valley halfway between Chepstow and Monmouth. Turning into the drive she switched on the car's headlights, for the tall beech trees on either side made their own twilight. When a gentle curve in the drive brought the old, stone-built house into sight, Fran stopped the car. As a child, she had spent many happy holidays with Gran and looking at the familiar outline of the trees, she felt a twinge of guilt.

The Court wasn't all that far away from Bristol yet she hadn't been up since Gran had decided to open the house and gardens.

It wasn't a large, grand house but dating back several hundred years it had been caught up in the history of the area. It had survived the early conflict between England and Wales before they were united, and then the Civil War, but one conflict it could not survive without drastic action was the cost it took to maintain.

Fran drove on slowly, but then had to brake sharply as a man on a bicycle pedalled furiously across the drive in front of her, his dark hair glinting in the car's headlights. Alarmed, she sounded the car horn, but the cyclist had already disappeared into the trees. Hands white-knuckled on the steering-wheel, tears blurred her vision. But these were the tears she should have shed after she had discovered Geoff and Anita. Instead, she had bottled up her anger and hurt over his betrayal. To have given vent to her emotions even in private would be admitting Geoff still had power over her, the power to hurt. But she mustn't arrive at The Court looking unhappy so, hastily brushing away the tears, she took a deep, calming breath.

She drove faster now, eager to reach the sanctuary of The Court. The car had hardly come to a stop in the cobbled kitchen yard before Mrs Bowen, the grey-haired, middle

4

aged housekeeper, came hurrying out.

'Oh, Fran, I'm so glad to see you! What with your gran's fall and those people wandering about trying to look busy—I haven't the slightest idea what they should be doing, and by the look of them, they don't seem to know either!'

'I think one of them certainly doesn't seem to know how to ride a bike safely! I nearly ran him over.'

She tried to sound casual but suddenly the enormity of the task ahead of her seemed to press Fran back into her seat. The last thing she wanted was the responsibility of seeing that the work continued during Gran's absence. If Geoff had managed to pull the wool over her eyes with such ease, then the people working in The Court wouldn't have any problem in taking advantage of the situation. But Mrs Bowen was opening the car door, almost pulling Fran out.

'Come on in! The sooner you get to grips with things the better. I'm not at all sure the upholsterer should have taken away so many chairs yesterday. Your grandmother complains she can't make ends meet, then lays out thousands just so strangers can tramp all over the place.'

Wearily Fran followed the housekeeper into the welcoming warmth of the large kitchen. But when Mrs Bowen looked at her searchingly, she pleaded tiredness, refusing all

5

offers of food and drink and escaped to the haven of her old bedroom. Switching on the light and glimpsing her reflection in the long mirror, she smiled mirthlessly. Large brown eyes smudged with dark shadows looked back at her, her skin sallow from lack of sleep. Swinging her hold-all on to the blanket chest at the foot of the bed, she told herself firmly that coming to The Court was the complete break she needed.

Fran slept fitfully that night, her dreams disturbing. A cynical, laughing Geoff was the main character, but the setting was The Court. Waking early and seeing the morning sun brightening her room, she got up and scrambled into her track suit. Back home, she often started the day with a run, and hopefully here, the clean air and peacefulness would help to clear her head.

Slipping quietly out of the kitchen, she decided to keep to the large gardens. Heading towards the lavender-hedged rose garden, she stopped in amazement as she saw the transformation. Taking in the neatly-clipped lavender and the exuberant roses now pruned into shape, she realised how the garden had been left very much to its own devices in the last few years.

'You approve?'

The speaker's silent approach had her turning around in annoyed surprise.

'What do you mean, creeping up on me like

6

that?' she demanded, looking up at him, a hand over her thumping heart.

The tall man now standing facing her seemed vaguely familiar. Dressed in clothes which had seen better days, his skin had been browned by constant exposure to the elements. Of course, he was the man on the bike!

'It was you who cycled in front of my car last night. It's a good job my brakes are efficient,' she exclaimed.

As a slow grin spread infuriatingly across his face, she added sharply, 'It isn't funny!'

'I know, I'm sorry,' he apologised. 'I was in a hurry.'

'You looked as though the devil was after you.'

'Not the devil.'

He left unsaid the true reason. Then lifting a hand in brief farewell, he walked swiftly away in the direction of the kitchen garden, whistling softly. It took all her resolve to stay where she was until he was out of sight, for her first impulse had been to run back into the house and question Mrs Bowen about him. She was puzzled by the niggling feeling that he was familiar. Could she have seen him years ago when staying with her grandmother? In her early teens a man ten years older than her would have seemed too ancient to notice properly. But now in her early twenties, his obvious attractiveness had disturbed her.

Back in the empty kitchen, Fran prepared

her usual breakfast of cereal and orange juice. She could hear Mrs Bowen opening and shutting doors and guessed the housekeeper was keeping an eye on what was happening in the rooms which were to be open to the public. Fran sighed. After breakfast she would have to get to grips with things, get to know the various contractors. It was all so new to her and she hoped she was up to it all for she did not want to keep phoning her grandmother.

Taking her breakfast to the well-scrubbed pine table, she sat down facing the door into the house. She had always liked this kitchen, the gleam of old copper saucepans, the well-polished Welsh dresser laden with china, the Aga, so warming.

Fran was just draining the last drops of her orange juice when she heard the back door open. Stifling a sigh, she turned around. She had hoped to have a little time to look around before meeting the people involved with the restoration. Pinning on a smile as she turned, it turned to a frown when she saw the fair-haired man enter.

'What do you want?' she asked. 'If you've a problem . . .'

'No problem,' he replied coolly, 'unless you've eaten all the bacon.'

Fran's mouth dropped open in astonishment as, walking to the sink, he washed his hands. Following him, she put her bowl and glass noisily on to the draining board.

'What did you mean about the bacon?' she demanded.

If the workmen had become this free and easy during Elizabeth's short absence, then it was a good job she had come. Almost lazily he reached for the towel to dry his hands, his unconcern fuelling Fran's annoyance, putting a glint in her brown eyes. But impervious to this, he ignored her question.

'Mrs Bowen usually cooks me breakfast, but as she isn't here I'll do it myself. Care to join me in a fry-up?' he asked, going into the walk-in larder.

'I've had breakfast already,' Fran replied stiffly.

His silence irritating her, she followed him as far as the larder door, watching him choose an egg from a bowl, whistling quietly, as though he hadn't a care in the world. He seemed to be intent on annoying her.

Her voice edged with sarcasm, she said, 'You seem to be at home here.'

Head bent to look in the fridge for bacon, he did not answer immediately.

Then just as she began to say, 'Who . . .' he straightened up.

'Who am I?' he finished for her, brown eyes alight with amusement.

'You obviously find the situation amusing,' she said, then thinking it was time she made herself known, she added, 'I'm Frances Marchant. Elizabeth Merchant is my . . .'

9

'Grandmother,' he finished.

'Do you always complete people's sentences?'

For a moment he frowned as though making certain of his reply.

'No, I don't think I do. It's just that Elizabeth has talked about you.'

'Talked about me to you?'

Her voice rose with incredulity. Surely her grandmother hadn't told this workman about Geoff?

'Oh, you know how it is. Elizabeth and I seemed to hit it off straight away. We always begin discussing work and then find we've strayed on to other things. Now, if you'll excuse me, I'll get on with cooking my breakfast.'

Fran had intended standing firm, blocking his exit from the larder, but as he drew closer, determined on squeezing past her, she moved away.

'My grandmother hasn't mentioned by name anyone working here,' she went on, giving an invitation for him to introduce himself.

'I'm Ivo Heath,' he said going towards the stove.

'So, Ivo Heath, exactly what are you doing here? And I don't mean getting breakfast.'

'He's seeing to the garden,' a voice explained from the back door.

'Lisa! Thank goodness you've arrived,' Fran

said smiling with relief as a slightly-built, dark-haired girl came hurrying in. 'I was beginning to think I was in the wrong house.'

Fran knew Lisa slightly having met her a couple of times, but Elizabeth sometimes mentioned her, how plucky she was facing up to life after her husband's death and with the responsibility of having two small children. When needed, Lisa came in to help Elizabeth with letters, bills and accounts.

'I don't know if Elizabeth has told you, but now there's so much correspondence, I come in as often as I can, to help with the office side of things. Although I've tried to show her how to use it, Elizabeth won't even touch the computer!'

Some of Fran's worries disappeared as she said, 'Thank goodness, you'll know what's going on around here. Gran told me absolutely nothing when she phoned from the hospital. To start with, who is he?' Fran asked quietly, nodding towards the man now busy with a frying pan.

'Why, he's Ivo Heath,' Lisa said with surprise, then added with obvious admiration, 'You know, the famous garden designer.'

But instead of being impressed, Fran asked Ivo, 'Why the mystery? Why didn't you tell me who you were?'

'You never asked,' the mild reply came.

'It would have been good manners to have introduced yourself.'

'It was amusing to see you didn't know me,' he replied, hacking off a thick slice of bread, and putting it in the frying pan. 'You know, Fran, you really should begin the day with a good breakfast. Then you might not get rattled so easily.'

'I am not rattled!'

But she didn't get a chance to go on for Lisa was pulling her urgently towards the door into the house.

'Please, Fran, there's so much to talk about and I've got to leave at twelve to take Tom to the dentist. Ivo can bring you up to date with his plans for the garden later.'

'I might see you at lunch time,' Ivo said, intent on the contents of the frying pan. 'Mrs Bowen generally makes me sandwiches.'

Needled by the fact that Ivo Heath seemed to have the upper hand, Fran replied tartly, 'As you seem to spend most of your time eating, I shall be interested to see exactly how much you have accomplished so far in the garden.'

Following Lisa through to the hall, Fran muttered none too quietly, 'Round one to me I think, Mr Ivo Heath!'

Although Ivo didn't hear her, he was frowning as he sat down to eat.

CHAPTER TWO

'If you don't mind me saying,' Lisa said, leading the way into what used to be the breakfast room, but was now Elizabeth's study, 'you shouldn't speak to Ivo like that. Elizabeth was very lucky to get him.'

'She's no doubt paying him well,' Fran retorted. 'Just because he's good at his job doesn't give him the right to be so, so . . .'

But she didn't finish the sentence for, entering the study, she saw to her alarm that the IN-tray was piled high.

'Has all of this just come in since Elizabeth's fall?' she asked.

'No, but you know what she's like. She would rather be with the people doing the work. She likes to be involved.'

'Who's working here now, besides that is, the great Ivo Heath?'

Hearing Fran's barbed comment, Lisa looked at her reproachfully before answering, 'Most of the work has been completed, except for the odd thing. But Elizabeth still hadn't got around to going up into the attics to look for anything of interest which she could put in the rooms open to the public.'

'If Gran isn't back in time to do that, I shall enjoy rooting around in the attics,' Fran said. 'I used to love playing up there when I was little.'

Lisa shuddered.

'Didn't it frighten you? I hate it, all those dark, dingy rooms filled with dusty piles of goodness knows what.'

'That's exactly why I did like it. I never knew what I'd find. But I'll go up there when I've cleared all this paperwork. Now, what needs to be done first?' Fran asked.

Both standing by the leather-topped desk, Lisa went swiftly and efficiently through the paperwork, sorting out the things which needed immediate attention. Then reminding Fran that her office was only next door, Lisa told her to shout when she was ready to dictate any letters.

'Oh, there's no need for that,' Fran replied. 'I'm used to computers so I can do the letters myself.'

'It's my job,' Lisa replied stiffly. 'Elizabeth said her time was better spent supervising whatever was going on in the house.'

'Of course, how silly of me!' Fran said quickly. 'The work here is so different to what I've been doing, I might need a lot of help.'

Although she breathed a sigh of relief as, with a smile, Lisa left the room, Fran was cross with herself. She should have remembered Lisa needed the work, the money. Being a widow with two small sons couldn't be easy.

It was well over an hour before Fran finally had the paperwork into some sort of order, but instead of shouting for Lisa, she went to the

14

office. Opening the door, her smile died as she saw Ivo leaning over Lisa's shoulder, a brightly-coloured plant catalogue open on the desk in front of them. Hearing the door open, they both looked up, startled. Was it her imagination, Fran wondered, or did they both look guilty.

But in a trice Ivo straightened up, smiling as he said, 'Good morning.'

'Sorry if I disturbed you,' she said, not looking directly at either of them, then ignoring Ivo, she asked Lisa if she was ready to answer a few letters.

'Of course!' Lisa replied, trying to open a desk drawer.

'Is that stuck again?' Ivo asked.

He dropped down on his haunches to look at it. When a few sharp tugs freed it, he stood up.

'I'm sorry, I should have seen to it by now. I'll come back later.'

'There's no need for you to concern yourself,' Fran said smoothly. 'Mending drawers isn't part of your job and I'm sure you have plenty to do outside.'

With an amused shrug, Ivo left, but Lisa wasn't so easily dealt with.

'Fran, I know I'm only the secretary around here, but I've got to have my say. What on earth is the matter that you go on at Ivo like you do? Just now, he was only being helpful. Unless you've been living in some remote

15

corner of the world, you must know Ivo has a tremendous reputation as a garden designer, so why be so rude to him? Have you met him before and he offended you in some way?'

Fran frowned, puzzled.

'No, I don't think I have, yet there's something familiar about him.'

'I know we can all take an irrational dislike to someone, but I can't begin to tell you how he's gone out of his way to help Elizabeth, and he has such a way with children.'

'Your children, you mean?'

Lisa nodded and, seeing her eyes misting with tears, Fran put a comforting arm around her.

'I'm sorry. I really will try to get on with him. I didn't realise you and he were friendly.'

'He helps me with the boys. Since Alan died, Tom has become very unruly. Even Elizabeth couldn't get through to him. But Ivo, well, Tom seems to respect him. He's nearly back to the happy child he was before Alan was killed. But enough of my troubles. You've some correspondence for me.'

It was nearly noon before Fran left Lisa, and during that time she soon realised there was more to running The Court than just answering letters. On several occasions, Lisa suggested changes to what Fran had intended saying in a letter. Elizabeth, it seemed, had made friendly contacts, rather than the business-like ones Fran was used to.

'Does Gran know the private lives of everyone she deals with?' Fran asked incredulously. 'How on earth did she find out this plumber had a puppy who was chewing everything within sight?'

'Well, that's Elizabeth for you. She seems to invite confidences.'

'And what has she found out about Ivo Heath?'

Fran was nearly as startled by the question as Lisa was.

Hurriedly, she added, 'Not that it's any concern of mine.'

Seeing Fran's curiosity as a sign that she was softening towards Ivo, Lisa smiled but nevertheless had to admit that nothing much was known about his private life, except he was unmarried and lived for his work.

That evening, Fran ate a solitary meal in the small room Elizabeth had turned into a cosy dining-room. The impressive, large dining-room which had caused Fran to hate mealtimes as a child was now set out as though for a formal dinner for the benefit of visitors. Insisting she wanted only a light meal, Fran told Mrs Bowen to take the evening off. At first the housekeeper had been reluctant but then confessed there was a good film she wanted to see in Bristol and as Ivo was going to the city, too, he had offered to take her and bring her back.

Sitting at the table which overlooked the

neglected herb garden, Fran wondered what Ivo was doing in Bristol. Had he a girlfriend there? Then she shook her head as though to banish such silly thoughts. What was it to her what he did with his free time? But try as she might, every strand of her thoughts kept coming back to him. But as she served herself a generous helping of Mrs Bowen's delicious kiwi pavlova, she resolved to put Ivo out of her mind.

Tired by learning a totally new job, Fran went to bed early. But she slept so lightly that she heard Ivo's car return and the back door open and close. Mrs Bowen's room was reached by the back stairs and Fran heard them creak as they had always done. Even though she knew the housekeeper to be in her room, Fran still listened, but there was no other sound. She had never thought to ask if there was anyone else living in the house, other than herself and the housekeeper, but if Ivo didn't sleep in The Court, where did he sleep? Then just as swiftly as the question had popped into her mind, she dismissed it firmly. Where he lived was no concern of hers.

The next morning, Fran was up early and as she always liked to begin the day silently, she took her breakfast into the study. She had not gone for her morning run in case she met Ivo, telling herself this was because she wanted to avoid the prickly atmosphere which seemed to have sprung up between them. Denied her

18

exercise, she was now trying to massage away the resulting headache. Although she knew she was being petty, she blamed Ivo for it, for a run around the grounds would have left her clear-headed.

Her breakfast finished, Fran turned her attention to the wallpaper sample book from which she had to choose the wall covering for the final area to be renovated, the stairs and corridor leading to the attics. Although visitors would not be allowed up there, Elizabeth had decided that as the rest of the house had been given a make-over, this little-used corridor should as well. Flipping through the pages, Fran could not see even one paper which pleased her and yet she had to choose by lunch time, for the decorators were eager to finish.

With a sigh, she picked up the heavy book and carried it up the back stairs. The windowless attic corridor ran the whole length of the house, with rooms leading off on both sides. Wanting to see the samples in daylight rather than electric light, she opened the farthest door, letting sunlight shaft across the corridor. In doing so, her eye was caught by an old dolls' house and rocking horse standing forlornly amongst an untidy pile of battered old books. A sudden pang of nostalgia took her into the room, where she ran a fond hand over the rocking horse.

Elizabeth had kept all of the toys which had enchanted many Marchant children over the

19

years. Now there was only Fran left and in the mood she was in after Geoff's unfaithfulness, it would be a long time before she would have children.

'Poor Dapple,' she murmured into the horse's dusty mane.

'Sorry to interrupt your conversation with the rocking horse.'

With an exclamation of alarm, Fran turned.

'What are you doing here?' she demanded of Ivo, who was leaning against the door frame, arms folded.

How long had he been there, she wondered.

'Elizabeth said there was a book of old garden plans up here, but she fell before she could find it. So as she has asked me to restore the garden to what it was about one hundred years ago, I thought I'd try to find the plans for that time.'

Brushing down her dusty skirt, Fran remarked, 'You've left it a bit late, haven't you?'

'Oh, you mean that I've already made a start on the garden?'

Pushing himself away from the door frame, Ivo went towards the pile of old books and, dropping down on his haunches, opened the first one.

Annoyed by his apparent dismissal of her presence, Fran asked with a humourless smile, 'What have you used up to now? A crystal ball?'

'No,' Ivo replied evenly. 'Elizabeth knew some areas, like the rose garden, hadn't been changed much. So all I will have to do there in the autumn is replant where necessary, with old-fashioned roses.'

'You're going to be here that long?'

Fran had moved to the door, but still Ivo hadn't looked up. He sounded distracted as though thinking of other things.

'No, I've other projects to check on during the summer. I've arranged with your grandmother that after this initial work, I shall come back when necessary.'

Fran was annoyed she hadn't known this, but then why should she, when she had shown little interest in The Court's restoration?

'Who will keep the lawns mown and flower beds weeded during your absence?'

Closing the first book before putting it down carefully on the dusty floorboards, it was a few long seconds before he explained.

'I've taken on a couple of local men to see to general maintenance and, of course, I will be keeping an eye on things.'

'I haven't seen any sign of gardeners, other than you.'

'There's no reason why you should, unless your early morning run takes you farther out into the grounds where they are waging war on rhododendrons. But you must have been about early this morning for you had obviously breakfasted. Where did you jog today?'

He looked up at her and even in the gloom the intensity of his gaze caught her by surprise.

'I didn't go this morning.'

He raised an eyebrow in silent questioning, but she refused to be drawn. Suddenly wanting the sanctuary of the study, she was halfway down the corridor before she realised she had left the wallpaper book behind in the attic. Frowning, she hurried back to the study.

Opening the door, a waft of heady perfume drew her eyes to a blue bowl of perfect white hyacinths on the window sill. Going over to admire them, she wondered whether it was Lisa or Mrs Bowen who had put them there. Whoever it was, she must remember to thank them later.

CHAPTER THREE

'Have you chosen that wallpaper yet?' a man in paint-smudged white overalls asked as he came into the study.

'Yes, I have,' Fran fibbed swiftly, annoyed with herself that she had let Ivo rattle her so she had left the sample book in the attic. 'I'll just fetch the book. I'll only be a minute.'

As the decorator sighed, Fran ran up to the attics. Now she would have to choose a paper quickly instead of taking her time to find just the one of which her grandmother would approve. But as she reached the beginning of the corridor, Ivo came hurrying out of the attic room with the sample book.

'I was just coming for that,' Fran exclaimed. 'The decorator is waiting for my decision about the paper for this corridor and stairs.'

'In that case you had better choose quickly,' Ivo said, helpfully holding open the heavy sample book. 'Do you want something in keeping with the age of the house which might be dark and heavy looking, or something light and modern?'

'I don't know,' Fran said vaguely, hastily flicking over pages. 'I wonder what Gran would have chosen,' she murmured to herself.

'Although Elizabeth was restoring the rooms she intended opening to the public in the way they would have looked many years ago, I always felt she was very young at heart, willing to consider newer things.'

Stung by the fact that Ivo seemed to be hinting he knew Elizabeth's tastes better than she did, Fran pushed the book towards him.

'In that case, you had better choose the paper.'

Seeming not to have noticed her annoyance, he swiftly leafed through the pages until he came to a paper with sunny yellow stripes on a white background.

'There, how about that?' he asked, looking down the corridor as though already seeing the paper there. 'It's bright without being garish and the simple pattern will give a feeling of space.'

Grudgingly, Fran nodded her head. Ivo was right, it would look good.

'Right then, I'll carry the book down for you. It's quite heavy.'

Even though he was carrying the book, Ivo turned to close the door of the attic which held the rocking horse and books. Although he was between her and the door, Fran caught a glimpse of untidiness as though he had been searching frantically for something. Was it the mess he didn't want her to see, or didn't he want her asking awkward questions? Before she could ask him, Ivo was hurrying away. Reaching the study, he put the sample book down on the desk and with a swift nod to the decorator, left.

That lunchtime, Fran cautiously peeped around the kitchen door, and seeing the sole occupant was Mrs Bowen, she went in.

'I haven't got your lunch ready yet,' Mrs Bowen flustered. 'That decorator can't half talk when he's a mind to, but when he wants to get on, he can be really quick.'

'He'll soon be gone,' Fran tried to pacify. 'Then the house will be back to normal.'

'That will never be. There'll be hordes of gawping tourists.'

'Hardly hordes. The Court isn't a stately home.'

'You're half wrong. It might not be stately,

24

but it is a home, well, of sorts, for what this house craves is a young family.'

Before the housekeeper launched into commenting that what was needed first was a wedding, Fran tried to turn the conversation.

'Was it you or Lisa who put those lovely hyacinths in the study?'

'Oh, that will have been Ivo. One of the first things he did was to repair one of the old greenhouses. He's been growing bowls of bulbs there as well as raising flower seedlings. Proper green fingers he's got.'

In which case, Fran thought with relief, he would be putting bowls of bulbs all over the house. As her bowl was one of many, there would be no need for her to thank him.

Having managed to avoid Ivo for the rest of the day, that evening Fran decided to walk around the herb garden behind the house, for some fresh air and exercise. The layout of the herb garden had remained virtually unchanged over the years and so Fran knew her way along the narrow paths which separated the numerous beds. As she strolled along, she was saddened to see the neglect.

Reaching the centre where several paths met at a huge lead urn, Fran reflectively ran her hand around its fluted edge. When her grandfather had been alive, she could remember it being planted with masses of trailing plants, but since his death several years ago, Elizabeth had not had the money to employ men other than part-time, and this only to do what was really necessary. Now she was having to pay greatly for Ivo Heath's work.

'Penny for them.'

Fran heard the crunch of his feet on the gravelled path just before Ivo spoke. Fran glanced up at him, her face expressionless.

'When you know what I was thinking, you might withdraw your offer.'

'Ah, so without sounding conceited, I guess you were thinking about me, and none too favourably.'

Bending to copy her posture, he looked across at her, smiling wryly. His nonchalant manner ruffling her, Fran did not bother to be tactful.

'I was thinking your huge fee would have paid the wages of several gardeners for quite some time.'

'What Elizabeth is paying me is between the two of us and she seems more than happy with our arrangement.'

He frowned as his gaze swept over the herb garden.

'It really is time I got round to doing something with this though.'

'I'm willing to tackle it.'

Fran was astonished to hear herself volunteer swiftly. Then so Ivo would not think she was offering to help him, she went on quickly.

'It's something I would like to do in memory

of my grandfather. He was a keen gardener and loved the herb garden.'

'That's fine by me,' Ivo agreed, straightening up.

'You don't mind?'

'I'm not one of those professionals who keeps the eager amateur at bay. In fact if you press the right button, I can go on and on about gardening.'

'Even if you're not being paid?' Fran said automatically.

As soon as she had spoken, Fran regretted it. Ivo had willingly agreed to her restoring the herb garden and yet she had not missed the opportunity to try to needle him again about his fee. When he did not reply, she hurriedly filled in the silence with a hasty thanks for the hyacinths.

'It was no bother at all. I'm glad you liked them. It seems Lisa can't stand the scent of hyacinths.'

As he walked away with just a wave for goodbye, Fran felt strangely rebuffed. So the hyacinths had been rejected by Lisa, and Ivo had no doubt put them in the study rather than take them back to the greenhouse. Her mouth clamped into a hard line. Geoff had made it very plain she was second best, and now, though in a minor way, she had been second best yet again. If this was not to be the pattern of her life, then she would have to do something about it.

Relaxing next evening in the cosy sitting-room Elizabeth used when by herself, Fran decided the way to prevent being second best was to be more assertive. This meant she would have to stop worrying about meeting Ivo. Geoff had let her down romantically, but Ivo was only someone employed by Elizabeth and so her dealings with him were purely about his work. Having made this decision, she realised she hadn't felt so relaxed for several weeks.

Her romance with Geoff had not been all sunshine and roses. How many times had she lain awake worrying about him and how to please him? If she hadn't spent so much time looking ahead but had concentrated on the present, might she have noticed the growing attraction between him and Anita? Then suddenly Fran smiled. Elizabeth often accused her of crossing bridges before she came to them, so what would she say about Fran looking back? Wasn't there some saying about burning your bridges so there was no going back?

She didn't hear the light tap on the door and as Ivo came in, she looked up with eyes unfocused by her thoughts.

'Sorry, did I frighten you? I did knock,' he said softly.

'I was day dreaming,' she said, excusing her flustered state, before adding a little breathlessly, 'Come in and sit down.'

She smiled slightly, not quite in welcome, but with relief. The first step in being more positive had been easy. If Ivo was surprised by her friendliness, he did not show it as he sank with a tired sigh into the comfortable armchair opposite her. It was then Fran noticed he was holding a book.

'Is that what you were looking for in the attic?' she asked, leaning forward to try to read the title on the spine.

'No, this is for you. I thought you might find it helpful. It's a history of herb gardens and what was grown in them.'

As he held out the leather-bound volume, Fran took it with a smile of thanks and began to flip through the pages, exclaiming as beautiful pictures of flowers caught her eye. Then suddenly aware Ivo was watching her intently, she closed the book.

'Did you find the plans you were looking for up in the attic?'

'Er, no,' he replied vaguely, then turned to go so suddenly that Fran was startled. 'I'd better be going. I haven't tidied my place for several days and Mrs Bowen is bound to call with some of her home cooking for me. Then she goes on about me coming to live here where she can take care of me.'

'You don't strike me as a man who needs taking care of,' Fran said, looking in his direction, but avoiding any direct eye contact. 'By the way, where do you live?'

'I've made myself very comfortable in the lodge by the top gate.'

'So that was where you were going the other evening when you pedalled so furiously across the drive.'

'Yes, I'd spent longer than I'd intended at Lisa's.'

As Ivo left, Fran felt unhappiness beginning to ooze through her body. With sudden determination, she headed for the kitchen. A cup of tea would stop her self-pity. After all, she couldn't go through life begrudging others their happiness, especially Lisa.

CHAPTER FOUR

During the next few days Fran had no time to worry about either Geoff or Ivo for she was busy checking that renovations, repairs and upholstery had been completed satisfactorily. Most of the men involved, knowing Fran was standing in for Elizabeth, said it did not matter if the final inspection was left until a later date. But Fran wanted as much as possible to be finalised so when Elizabeth returned, there would be less for her to do.

Even though Lisa did as much as she could to help, Fran worked far into the evenings. Some of the time was spent writing up the day book she had started so Elizabeth could look back to discover what had been happening in her absence. Fran intended taking the day book when she visited Elizabeth, for besides being a record of happenings, it hopefully would show everything was under control.

'I wondered what you were up to,' Ivo said, coming into the study early one evening. 'The sun's still shining and it's such good growing weather you can almost hear the plants shooting up.'

Turning away from the computer, Fran massaged the band of tiredness pressing around her forehead.

'I'm glad everything is going well in your department,' she said wearily.

As Ivo leaned over her shoulder to look at the computer screen, a shiver swept up her back and, noticing the slight tremor, Ivo asked if she was cold.

'No, I'm not cold. It's what Gran used to call someone walking over your grave.'

Straightening, Ivo questioned sharply, 'Was it me? Were you reacting to my presence, to me being so close?'

'No, of course not,' Fran denied swiftly, but as she turned to face him with a pinned-on smile, she knew instinctively this was not so, but why was her sixth sense warning her to be on her guard?

Satisfied with her reply, Ivo urged, 'Why not leave things until tomorrow when Lisa can do them?'

'I can't leave everything to her. I'm already putting far more on Lisa than Gran would have done.'

'Lisa doesn't mind.'

'Have you been discussing me with her?' Fran demanded.

'Discussing is a little strong,' Ivo said. 'Of course we mention you. It would be odd if we didn't, considering we are all working together. Talking about work, how about tearing yourself away from the computer and coming for a walk with me? I'm not an ogre, you know.'

Glancing up at him, Fran's reply that she had a lot to do died on her lips. Under questioningly raised eyebrows, his eyes were of an incredible intense dark brown. Geoff had brown eyes.

'Don't look at me like a frightened rabbit,' he said, coming closer. 'Are you coming with me or not?'

Fran turned back to the computer vaguely muttering something about an urgent letter. As Ivo shut the door none too quietly behind him, she leaned back in her chair, a deep exhalation of breath a measure of her tension.

Glancing out of the window, she wished now she had gone with him. The fresh air and exercise would have done her good. Ivo had been right, she was acting like a frightened rabbit. Just because Geoff had brown eyes and had let her down didn't mean all brown-eyed men spelled trouble. But there was something about Ivo, something she couldn't quite put her finger on, but nevertheless warned her that she should be careful.

Fran had laughed when on her first morning at The Court, Mrs Bowen insisted on handing over Elizabeth's huge bunch of keys. But the housekeeper was adamant that she did not want the responsibility of anything going missing. Putting them in a drawer in her desk, Fran had not had need of them until next morning when an electrician said he wanted to give a final check to the wiring in the cellar.

Over the years, her grandfather had laid down many bottles of fine wine, and carrying on the habit of past owners of The Court had kept the cellar locked. But when Fran opened the desk drawer where she kept the keys, they were not there. Thinking she had absentmindedly put them in another drawer, she searched, but there was no sign of them. Then assuming Mrs Bowen must have borrowed them, Fran went into the kitchen.

'No, I've told you, I want nothing to do with those keys,' the housekeeper said. 'And when you do find them, don't you go leaving that electrician alone in that wine cellar.'

Going back to the study, Fran apologised to the electrician, and asked him if there was something else he could do whilst she hunted for the keys. With an amiable nod, he set off towards the kitchen, no doubt to ask Mrs

Bowen for a brew. Fran methodically emptied each drawer then she looked under the desk and searched the filing cabinet but to no avail. Had a workman, knowing where the keys were kept, borrowed them without asking? With a frown of worry, she went in search of anyone who might have done so, but quickly drew a blank for there was only a handful of people still working at The Court.

Really worried by now, Fran pondered what to do as she walked back to the study. She could change the locks but it would be very expensive.

She was just going past the library, when she heard the squeak of a protesting hinge and knew this meant someone was opening the old glass-paned doors of the numerous book cabinets. Fran pushed open the library door. Looking back on it later, she didn't know who had been the most startled, her or Ivo. But she did remember that she had demanded, not asked what he was doing there.

'I told you up in the attic, I'm looking for old books about the house and its gardens.'

She noticed he seemed to be avoiding looking at her, but why, when looking in the library was the obvious thing to be doing? After all he was restoring the gardens. Then she saw the bunch of keys lying on the table.

'Why did you take the keys without asking me first?' she asked crossly. 'I've been looking for them everywhere. The electrician wants to

34

go down into the cellar.'

'You weren't about. I didn't think you would mind.'

Swiftly picking up the keys, he turned to lock the doors he had opened.

'Sorry about that,' he said, hurrying past her. 'As it's my fault, I'll find the electrician and give him the keys.'

She didn't have a chance to reply, and it was only then she noticed that in his other hand, held close to his body, there were several sheets of paper. Surely he hadn't torn them out of a book? But before she could call after him, he had gone. Hurrying to the bookshelves, Fran hastily checked through the few volumes that seemed as though they might have something to do with The Court, but she found no pages missing. But what she did find between two books was an old, empty folder. Checking to see if there were any clues to its contents, she sighed heavily when she found nothing. Had Ivo taken whatever it had held? And how, she wondered, would Elizabeth have dealt with such a problem.

Now that The Court was nearly ready for the opening, Fran felt she could visit Elizabeth with a clear conscience. Although she was out of bed, sitting by a window, her grandmother's wan looks shocked Fran. But nevertheless, Elizabeth was eager to hear all about The Court. But when Fran casually asked Elizabeth how well she knew Ivo, her grandmother frowned and when she did reply, she seemed to be considering every word.

'Why? Ivo is well respected. He's one of the best and I fully approve of his plans.'

'It's not that. The gardens are beginning to look good even though there's not much in flower yet. I just wondered how well you knew him as a person.'

'What a strange thing to ask. What's going on with you and Ivo?'

Elizabeth's tone held the edge of sternness Fran had known as a child to be indicating slight disapproval. To hide her confusion, she got up to move the bowl of hyacinths Ivo had sent.

'Oh, do stop fiddling about with that bowl. If you and Ivo have fallen out, then you will have to sort it out by yourself. Though I really can't imagine anyone failing to get on with that young man.'

'We've not fallen out. It's just that I was curious about his background.'

'Ah.' Elizabeth smiled knowingly. 'So you're wondering if there's a girlfriend in the background.'

'No, I am not! It's just, well, useful if you know more about people you work with, other than the job they're doing.'

'That didn't do you much good with Geoff, did it? How long had you been going out with him before you discovered he was a womaniser?'

Seeing Fran's cheeks redden with the anger she still harboured about Geoff, Elizabeth leaned over to pat her hand affectionately.

'Sorry, my dear, I shouldn't have said that. But I've always considered you a good judge of character and although I only met him a couple of times, I could never understand why you didn't see that young man for what he was.'

'Why didn't you say something?'

'Would you have listened?'

'I might.'

'Well, perhaps you will listen to me now. Ivo is a fine young man and don't you let memories of a bad experience go clouding your judgement about men.'

Folding her hands in her lap, as though closing a book, Elizabeth signalled that as far as she was concerned the subject of Ivo was over.

Fran had barely kicked off her shoes when she arrived home before the phone rang.

'How was Elizabeth? I expect you both talked your heads off,' Ivo said, laughing.

Although she knew it was unreasonable, such a swift call made her feel he had been watching for her return. How on earth had he known she was back when the lodge was some distance away, with many tall trees between them?

'Have you been perched in a tree with binoculars trained on The Court?' she asked, still feeling uneasy about the library incident.

Ivo replied mildly that it was a still evening and he had heard her car.

'I wasn't spying on you, if that's what you're thinking. I just wanted to know how Elizabeth was.'

'Sorry,' Fran muttered. 'I'm tired. Gran is fine, eager to know all about everything.'

'Did she approve of your choice of wallpaper for the attic corridor?'

She frowned, wishing she could see his expression. Was he looking anxious, wondering if she had really told Elizabeth everything . . . the scattered books in the attic . . . him taking the keys to the library and the missing papers.

'Yes, yes she did.' And then anxious to finish this hide-and-seek conversation she added, 'She was delighted with the hyacinths and very pleased that I'm going to try to restore the herb garden. Now if you don't mind, I'm very tired.'

She put the phone down before Ivo had time to ask anything else. However, she wasn't too tired to check that the house keys were still where she had hidden them in a carved, wooden box in the study. But to her alarm, they had gone. Rushing to the library, she bumped into Mrs Bowen.

'Whatever is the matter?' the housekeeper demanded. 'I knew something was amiss when I was dusting and found the house keys in that wooden box. Why on earth did you hide them there? Why didn't you lock them in a study drawer?'

'Those locks aren't very secure. Anyone could force them,' Fran said avoiding Mrs Bowen's curious eyes.

'If you mean me, then I'll have you know that over the years Elizabeth has trusted me with far more than a bunch of keys,' was the indignant reply.

'I'd trust you with the crown jewels.' Fran smiled, trying to lighten the atmosphere. 'But I didn't want to bother you. You weren't about.'

A little mollified, Mrs Bowen asked, 'Well, if it wasn't me, who were you hiding the keys from? Surely not Lisa?' Then seeing Fran shake her head, Mrs Bowen asked incredulously, 'Surely you don't think Ivo would go snooping about. Elizabeth trusted him, let him have the run of the place.'

Running her fingers through her hair, Fran mumbled, 'I've never had the responsibility of The Court before. There is so much of value here.'

'Then why didn't you take the keys with you?'

Fran shrugged, then asked brightly, 'How about a cup of tea while I tell you about Gran? She was delighted with the fruit cake you sent her.'

39

CHAPTER FIVE

Fran spent Sunday working hard in the herb garden, digging up weeds and cutting back straggly bushes. She hoped that by being very busy she would avoid further questioning by Mrs Bowen and also keep out of Ivo's way. If they did try to talk to her, she would use the gardening as a reason for not wanting to chat. But despite her resolve to concentrate on the herb garden, to the exclusion of all else, her thoughts wandered persistently.

Could Elizabeth be right about Geoff colouring her attitude towards men? But surely it was only natural. One day perhaps she would meet someone she could trust, but until then she would tread very carefully. And thinking about trust—was she reading too much into Ivo's behaviour in the attic and library? Was she seeing a mystery where there was none? Surely the way to banish any uncertainties about Ivo was to ask him, straight out. But suppose his movement had been quite innocent? That would leave her in a very awkward situation.

Standing up to ease a crick in her back and pushing back her hair, she reached a sudden decision. It was grossly unfair of her to lump Ivo in with Geoff. She would wipe the slate clean, begin afresh with Ivo.

40

On Sunday, the housekeeper normally cooked a big meal for one o'clock but that morning, Fran had asked her not to do so as she would not feel like working afterwards. After protesting that Elizabeth always enjoyed her Sunday dinner, Mrs Bowen grudgingly agreed to taking the afternoon off and at Fran's suggestion, went to see relatives in Chepstow.

By midday Fran's exertions had given her a large appetite so, leaving her mud-caked shoes by the back door, she washed her hands before going to see what the larder and fridge held. She was just putting the towel back, when Ivo came into the kitchen.

'What, no Sunday lunch?' he asked in surprise, making much of sniffing the air. 'Mrs Bowen isn't ill, is she? She seemed all right last night when she phoned to ask me to dinner today.'

To cover her confusion, Fran hurried towards the larder.

'No, she's fine,' she said over her shoulder. 'She must have forgotten. She's gone to Chepstow to visit her family.'

Her tone might have sounded casual, but she frowned as she wondered if Mrs Bowen's memory lapse had been nothing of the sort. Was the housekeeper trying to play cupid, leaving them together?

'How very odd,' Ivo said, following her. Then, 'Do you mind if I share something with you? The thought of one of Mrs Bowen's dinners has made me ravenous and I've nothing very substantial in my fridge.'

'What do you normally do on Sunday? Go for a pub lunch?'

'If Elizabeth doesn't ask me so we can discuss the garden whilst enjoying Mrs Bowen's excellent cooking, then I go to Lisa's.'

For a few seconds Fran's mind went blank. She hadn't realised Ivo and Lisa were that friendly. But then why should she? What did it matter to her?

'Are you all right?'

Ivo was so close that she felt his warm breath on the side of her face.

'Only your hand has been suspended over the cold chicken for ages. You haven't suddenly become a vegetarian, have you?'

'No.'

With an effort, Fran brought herself back to the present.

'I was just thinking Lisa might be expecting you.'

'She's taken the boys to visit Alan's parents. Seeing their grandsons helps to soften their grief a little. I don't know which is worse, losing a husband or a son. But you can't really measure anyone's grief, can you?'

'No, no you can't,' Fran said slowly.

Her hurt over Geoff was as nothing compared with Lisa's plight. Then picking up the plate with the chicken, she turned briskly to Ivo.

'Will you bring salad things from the fridge?'

'Yes, ma'am,' he replied, saluting her in mock subservience.

At Ivo's suggestion, they ate on a bench in the herb garden, backs against a sun-warmed house wall. As he had said, Ivo was indeed hungry and wasted no time in attacking his large plate of chicken salad. Fran was glad of this because she was still thinking about Lisa. Of course Lisa's life was far harder than hers. A rush of guilt suddenly closed Fran's throat and for a minute or two she was unable to swallow her food.

'Not hungry?'

With an effort Fran managed to swallow, then rushed into talking about the herb garden, anything to change the direction of her thoughts.

'It's taking me longer than I thought. There's so much to do.'

Ivo nodded. He knew only too well the many back-breaking hours involved in taming a garden which nature had reclaimed. But still not looking at Fran he asked softly, 'Did Elizabeth upset you yesterday? You've been miles away and the only thing that's happened recently is your visit to her.'

She shook her head vigorously in denial, and yet it had been Elizabeth who had started her thinking clearly.

43

'Then what?' His tone suddenly changing, Ivo said grimly, 'It isn't Geoff, is it? Has he contacted you, full of abject apologies?'

'How do you know about Geoff?' Fran demanded, turning to him.

'Mrs Bowen, and Elizabeth.'

'They had no right.'

'As your grandmother, Elizabeth only has your interest at heart. She didn't want me putting my big foot in it and I suppose the same could be said for Mrs Bowen.'

'Geoff is well and truly in the past.'

'I'm glad to hear it. You mustn't let philanderers like him ruin your future. Of course you can't wipe out a bad experience overnight, but you can try to replace it with something positive. Gardening is very therapeutic.'

'You, too?' she questioned softly.

'Me, too, but then there are very few people who haven't been hurt by a failed relationship. But listen to me, one minute I'm saying you should let the past go, the next I'm going on about it. I should practise what I preach. So whilst you go back to your gardening, I'll wash up.'

'What will you do then?'

Laying down her tray on the bench, Fran got up hurriedly. Had she really said that? She panicked. Her question sounded like the sort of thing an awkward teenager might say who wanted to be with a boy.

44

'I shall go into the wood and hack away some undergrowth.'

So that there was no doubt in Ivo's mind, Fran picked up her tray with, 'I'll help with the washing up then you can get to work that much sooner.'

'No!'

The sharpness of his reply surprising her, she said swiftly, 'I wasn't planning to give you the third degree about your past.'

'Sorry, I shouldn't have spoken like that. It shows I really do need to vent my anger on that undergrowth!'

As he took her tray, they both smiled, but it was hesitant, almost as though they were both asking for understanding. But what, Fran wondered, was Ivo angry about.

The following day, as always, Lisa came to the study to see what there was to do, but this time she seemed to want to chat and mindful of the strain she might be under, Fran leaned back in her chair, but before she could say anything, Lisa startled her.

'Isn't it odd that Mrs Bowen asked Ivo to lunch and then took the day off? She's not normally so absentminded,' Lisa said, putting down her notebook as she perched on the corner of the desk.

'We all forget things,' Fran answered.

'I expect you gave her the day off.'

The words hung in the air between them.

'Yes, but I didn't know Ivo was coming

45

here,' Fran replied hurriedly.

Was it her imagination or did Lisa looked relieved?

'Ivo often comes to us on Sunday,' Lisa said, intent on examining her nails. 'The boys really look forward to it. Since Alan died, they've been in sore need of a father figure.'

'I believe you go to see Alan's family regularly. I know it's no substitute but haven't the boys uncles or grandfathers?'

'Yes, but it isn't the same as having a man around on a day-to-day basis. Ivo kicks a football around with them, takes them fishing and sometimes lets them help him in the garden here.'

'Good, I'm glad. It must be hard for you.'

Fran trailed off, not knowing what to say next. Was Lisa warning her off? Was she thinking Fran had contrived to have a cosy lunch with Ivo?

'Right, Lisa, we had better get down to work. I want to keep up to date with the paperwork so when Gran comes home, I can go back to Bristol as soon as possible.'

This seemed to satisfy Lisa, for with a wide smile she picked up her notebook and asked Fran what needed attending to first.

Lisa might have gone away happy, but she left Fran feeling empty. But why? After all, Ivo was nothing to her. But why had she told Lisa she would be going back to Bristol when she really hadn't decided what she would do? The last thing she wanted was for Geoff to think she couldn't stay away from him. There she was thinking of him again, albeit in a negative way.

With a sigh, she was just reaching for a bank statement, when she heard Mrs Bowen laughing in the corridor leading to the kitchen.

'Now you look here, Ivo Heath, I've work to do even if you haven't.'

Although Fran could hear Ivo's deep voice, she couldn't catch what he was saying, but whatever it was, Mrs Bowen laughed again. Then there was a silence which had Fran straining her ears. Where was Ivo? Had he gone to see Lisa? Tight-lipped, Fran bent over the bank statement. Someone had to get on with the work, she thought dourly.

For such a big man, Ivo was surprisingly light on his feet and so Fran was not aware of his approach until he opened her door.

'Good morning, Fran,' he said cheerfully, but seeing her set expression he asked, 'Or isn't it a good one for you?'

'Yes, of course it is,' she replied swiftly.

She couldn't explain her downbeat feeling to herself, let alone Ivo.

'It's just that I hate checking bank statements, trying to make them tally with cheque books.'

'Then let Lisa do it,' Ivo said, coming to look over her shoulder. 'She will do it in a trice. She helped me once when I got in a

47

tangle.'

Fran felt herself unaccountably stiffen. What was the matter with everyone today? First Lisa, and now Ivo seemed to be intent on letting her know how close they were.

'I can manage,' she replied sharply.

But Ivo wasn't to be dismissed so easily.

'I see your IN-tray is empty, so before the postman comes with more mail for you, why not come and look around the garden with me, see what I've accomplished so far?'

'I've this statement,' she protested weakly, but her glance went to the window, to the sun shining enticingly in a sky of forget-me-not blue.

'Let Lisa do it,' he insisted firmly.

'No, I'll do it later.'

'Come on then,' Ivo urged, pulling her chair away from the desk.

But just as he did this, Fran began to stand up and, caught off balance, she staggered. Automatically Ivo reached out to steady her, but as she half turned to face him, he tightened his hold of her. For what seemed an eternity but was in fact seconds, they were so close that Fran was sure he would hear her wild heartbeat.

'Sorry, I seemed to lose my balance,' she murmured, not looking up.

'Fran?'

He said her name as a soft question and a shiver of unexpected pleasure thrilled through

48

her. Then as panic swept this away, she tried to pull free from his firm grasp.

His voice hardening, he demanded, 'What did that swine Geoff do to you that you fear being close to a man?'

'I'm not afraid,' she denied, looking anywhere but at him.

'Then look at me. Let me see you're not afraid to do even that.'

Slowly she lifted her face until she was looking at his firm chin, his mouth. Impatient to discover her true reaction mirrored in her eyes, he put a firm but gentle hand under her chin. She didn't immediately look at him, but then with the sudden resolve that Geoff was history, she met his gaze steadily.

'That's better,' he said, and when he made no attempt to draw closer, her mouth relaxed into the gentle curve of a half smile.

'Now, that's much better.'

Before she knew what was happening, his hands had dropped from her arms to her hands. She sensed he was watching her, waiting to see if she pulled away. But with a release of tension, she let her hands stay in his.

'I had better get a sweater,' she said a little unsteadily, but he kept holding her hands, seeming reluctant to let her go.

When he did slacken his fingers it was to slide slowly over the sensitive skin of her palms and with a small sigh, she closed her eyes. Suddenly letting her hands drop, he moved away.

'Here's your sweater,' he said, not looking at her as he grabbed it from a chair.

Startled, she took it from him. Why had his mood changed so suddenly? She hadn't said anything to offend him.

Going to the door, he urged, 'Let's look around the garden before the postman comes.'

Still a little dazed, Fran followed him. Once outside, Ivo's enthusiasm for the garden banished any lingering awkwardness between them. But Fran was left wondering if something in his past had caused his odd reaction to what could hardly be called an intimate moment.

CHAPTER SIX

Walking around the garden with Ivo, Fran felt as awkward and unsure as a young teenager. If she stood too close to him, would he think she was wanting closer contact? But if she kept away from him, would he think she was still smarting from Geoff, wanting to keep all men at a distance?

'Fran, is something wrong?'

They were standing in the sun-trap of the walled vegetable garden.

'Sorry! I think the warmth here has made me dozy,' she began.

'Let's go and sit in the shade over by the cut-flowers bed.'

'What do you mean by cut flowers?' she asked, following him to a simple bench hewn from a tree trunk.

'Elizabeth will need lots of flowers in the house when it's open and I'm doing what the old gardeners did, grow flowers in the vegetable garden where they can be picked without spoiling the layout of beds in the main part of the garden.'

'Oh, how lovely,' Fran said a little wistfully.

'Perhaps that could be one of your jobs here. I guess Elizabeth will not be able to walk much for a while.'

'I hadn't thought of that. How silly of me. She has always been so active I imagined that when she was out of plaster she would be her old brisk self.'

'So weren't you planning to stay long?'

Fran darted him a swift look. Was it her imagination that his voice seemed to hold a note of disapproval? Was he thinking she was uncaring about Elizabeth?

'Of course I'll stay as long as Gran needs me,' she rushed out. 'But then I'll have to look for another job.'

'In Bristol?'

'I haven't decided yet. I've friends there, but . . .'

'But you don't want to run into either Geoff or Anita.'

'How did you know her name?' Fran demanded, looking at him sharply.

Reaching over to pull up a weed, Ivo frowned.

'What does it matter how I knew the wretched girl's name? For goodness' sake, Fran, leave the past behind.'

'How can I when you all keep reminding me of it?' she accused. 'I mention Bristol and you immediately remind me of the two people I'm trying to forget.'

Cutting short his apology, she stood up with, 'I'd better get back. I've loads to do.'

Without looking at each other they both hurried off in opposite directions, Fran thinking grimly that if Lisa had indeed been warning her off Ivo, she had no need. She was more than welcome to him!

Having dodged both Mrs Bowen and Lisa, Fran hurried back to her study, slamming the door harder than she intended. But Mrs Bowen and Lisa both heard, the former tutting anxiously as she tried to think of a reason to see Fran. An ideal excuse came when the housekeeper answered the phone. It was Elizabeth and after the usual enquiries about Elizabeth's leg and Mrs Bowen's sciatica, Elizabeth asked to speak to Fran.

'You'll not find her in a good mood,' she was warned. 'She went out happily enough to look around the garden with Ivo, but then a few minutes ago, she came in by herself and from the way she banged the door, I guess she and Ivo have had a difference.'

Hearing Elizabeth's deep sigh, Mrs Bowen added hurriedly, 'But don't go fretting yourself. It will take Fran some time to get over that good-for-nothing Bristol fellow.'

But Elizabeth cut her short by asking her to put Fran on the phone.

'Hello, Gran, is everything all right?' Fran asked anxiously, but at the same time listening for the click which would indicate that Mrs Bowen had replaced the extension in the kitchen.

'Yes, I'm fine. But what's all this I hear about you and Ivo falling out?'

'Mrs Bowen certainly doesn't waste much time. She seems to forget I'm not a child and can handle my own problems.'

'She's known you since you were little and it's only natural that she is concerned.'

'What do I have to do? Get a plane to trail a banner across the sky saying that no man is worth losing sleep over?'

'Fran, calm down! It's understandable that you never want to see Geoff again, but don't let your hurt spill over into everyday life.'

'I don't know what Mrs Bowen has been saying to you, but it's hardly world-shattering news that Ivo and I sometimes don't see eye to eye.'

'I agree, unless, that is, it's the tip of the iceberg of distrust you've been towing behind

53

you ever since Geoff.'

'If one more person mentions Geoff this morning. I'll . . . I'll . . .'

'Fran, I have told Mrs Bowen to be careful what she says, to stop reminding you about him.'

'It wasn't her this time. It was Ivo.'

'Was it indeed? Now that is unexpected.'

'What do you mean?'

'Let's change the subject. I've rung to ask you to chase up the picture restorer. It's high time a cleaned-up Abigail was back in all her glory.'

'When visitors ask about her, will you tell them what a wicked woman she was? How many husbands did she push down the stairs?' Fran asked, thankful for the change of subject to a favourite portrait of an ancestor.

'It was all so long ago that things are a little vague. I think the number most often quoted is five.'

'It's no wonder she resorted to polishing the stairs. I would have done so a lot sooner!'

'Frances,' Elizabeth ordered sharply, 'if you continue with this silly distrust of men, then I'd better make arrangements to come home before you upset Ivo so much that he leaves.'

'Gran, I'm so sorry, really I am. Don't worry, I'll make an effort with Ivo. I've got to stop crossing my bridges before I come to them. I've been behaving like a schoolgirl thinking every boy she meets has designs on her.'

'And have you been thinking Ivo has designs on you?'

Even though her grandmother couldn't see her, Fran squirmed with embarrassment.

'No, of course not. I just put it awkwardly, that's all.'

When Elizabeth changed the subject yet again, asking how the herb garden restoration was going, Fran replied swiftly, tumbling out her sentences to prevent the conversation reverting to the one topic she wanted to avoid, Ivo.

And as though he wanted to avoid seeing Fran, Ivo kept well away from the house for the next few days.

It was late on Thursday evening, when Fran was kneeling in front of an old trunk in the attic, when Ivo came searching for her. Hearing him calling her name up the stairs, she held her breath. She had got into the habit of rummaging about looking for things which reminded her of happy childhood days and had just opened the lid of an old trunk. Rocking back on her heels, she frowned. What could he want with her this late in the day? Elizabeth's words about getting on with Ivo pricked Fran's conscience, yet part of her hoped he would go away.

Now he was calling out again and she bit her lip in frustration when she realised the corridor lights were on. Although she listened intently, she didn't hear him until he came through the door.

'At last, there you are,' he said, coming into the room. 'The attics are just the place to hide.'

'I wasn't hiding! I was just looking for things I used to play with.'

'Let's see,' he said, dropping down on his haunches by her side. 'Oh, dolls' house furniture. Dolls' houses fascinated me when I was a boy, but of course not having a sister I hadn't the chance to play with one.'

With a half smile, Fran watched as he bent over the trunk to lift out a tiny rocking chair. But when she found herself looking at his hair gleaming in the electric light, she was panicked into saying something, anything.

'Why did you hurtle in front of my car that first evening?' she asked.

'Well, someone has been coming into the garden at night and digging up the plants and smaller shrubs. I was on the point of catching whoever it was before the noise of your car scared them off.'

'Why on earth should they want to destroy the gardens? What has Elizabeth ever done to them?' Fran asked indignantly.

'They take the plants to sell, most probably miles away where they wouldn't arouse suspicion.'

'Can't the police do anything, keep watch?'

'Although they are sympathetic, they haven't

got the manpower.'

'Why didn't you tell me about this earlier? I could have kept a look-out.'

'That's the very reason why I didn't tell you, for I guessed you'd throw caution to the winds and go after them. I'm well able to look after myself,' he said softly.

'So am I,' she countered.

'Fran, I know this is the age of equality between the sexes, but you see, I'm old-fashioned. I feel women should be protected.'

'You mean tied to the kitchen sink.'

'Did I say that?' he asked.

Slowly his hand went to lift her chin. She sensed what he was going to do, but waited with breath held for the feel of his strong fingers on her face.

'Fran, if you don't stop being so prickly, I shall start calling you Mrs Tiggey Winkle, or whatever that hedgehog was called. Though now I come to think of it, I bet you would flare at the Mrs bit.'

'No, I wouldn't,' she said softly. 'After all she was only a nursery story character, and I'm . . . I'm . . .'

She trailed off uncertainly, but Ivo finished for her with, 'A very attractive woman.'

Slowly, as though not wanting to frighten her, he leaned closer and she felt confident enough to really look at him. His skin was tanned from the sun and wind, laughter lines radiated from the corner of his eyes, and as he drew closer, his hair flopped over his forehead. For the last few days, she might have succeeded in forgetting Geoff, but apprehension still lurked. Ivo kissed her gently and she responded slowly as though this was her first kiss. But before the kiss could deepen, he drew away slightly, murmuring, 'Let's take things slowly. There's no rush.'

'If you're thinking that it's too soon after Geoff . . .'

'Oh, not him again!'

Ivo let go of her so suddenly that she rocked back on to her heels. Swiftly, he stood up, hands on hips.

'The way you seem to cherish his memory, I'm beginning to think you would go back to him if he just whistled.'

'That's not true,' Fran denied hotly, scrambling to her feet. 'He's past history. It's you who keeps mentioning him.'

A shadow flickered so swiftly across Ivo's face, that later, looking back on what had happened, Fran wondered if she had imagined it.

'Perhaps we both need time,' he muttered slowly, turning away.

'Perhaps we do,' Fran agreed.

But Ivo was already going back down the corridor.

Fran didn't have long to think about what had happened, for as she reached the top of the attic stairs, she saw Mrs Bowen miming that she was wanted on the phone.

'Gran! Nothing's happened to her, has it?' she asked, hurrying down.

'No, it's Lisa. It seems her boys are ill.'

Going to the phone, Fran felt relieved to have something else to think about, other than Ivo.

'Lisa, I'm sorry to hear about the boys. What's the matter with them?'

'Chickenpox. I knew Ivo would forget to tell you, but that's men for you,' she said with a laugh. 'He said he would tell you straightaway, but perhaps something happened.'

Fran nodded. Yes, indeed, something had happened. So Ivo's reason for seeking her out hadn't been just for her company. But Lisa was speaking again, apologising that she wouldn't be able to come to work until the boys were better.

'After Ivo left me, I remembered a couple of things I haven't quite finished.'

Although Fran was taking in what Lisa was saying, a bit of her was wondering about Lisa's choice of words, 'Ivo left me.' Why hadn't she said 'us' or 'the house'? Did it mean that she considered Ivo to be very much part of her life?

CHAPTER SEVEN

It was on the second day of Lisa's absence from work that Fran ran into a problem she could not deal with. Normally she would have asked Lisa, who would know all the details of Elizabeth's dealing with a company supplying a cast-iron gazebo for the garden. Elizabeth had been precise in her instructions of its construction and Ivo had also supplied a drawing to scale, but the day after Elizabeth's fall, the company had sent a gazebo which did not fit the position for which it was destined.

The letter now lying in front of Fran contained veiled threats of wanting immediate payment, even though the gazebo had been returned to them as unsatisfactory. Getting up, Fran went into Lisa's small office and switched on the computer, but try as she might, she could not find any record of the correspondence which had been sent to the company, nor their replies in the filing cabinet. Although Fran did not have the time to spend in fruitless searching, she did not want to phone Lisa. When she had done so previously to ask about the boys, Lisa had sounded very fraught.

So with the faint hope that Mrs Bowen might have picked up something of what had passed between The Court and the now hostile company, Fran went in search of her.

Fran eventually ran the housekeeper to earth in the large walk-in airing cupboard, and in a few words, she outlined her problem. Mrs Bowen shook her head.

'Why should I know about such things? Thank goodness, outside is nothing to do with me. Have you asked Ivo?' Then seeing Fran's slight head-shake, she continued, 'I don't know which of you is the most touchy, you or Ivo. If it isn't you avoiding him, he's avoiding you. If you ask me, you both need a good shaking.'

'Well, I'm not asking you,' Fran replied sharply, but then had the grace to hurry out an apology.

Even though she was heavily burdened with inside work, Fran went into the herb garden where, for a few minutes, she dealt remorselessly with the remaining weeds, relieving her tension. But as she worked, her mind was awhirl with recent events. Why had she let Ivo kiss her? If she was honest, she knew she had been attracted to him. If she had not been so hurt by Geoff, she had the sneaking suspicion she might have fallen in love with Ivo. There was something about him. She sensed reliability, constancy, virtues which Geoff certainly had not possessed. But deny it as she might, there was a strong physical attraction, too, something she would have to guard against.

With an exasperated sigh, Fran marched off

in the direction of the kitchen garden, where she knew Ivo had been busy preparing beds for vegetables. But when she got there, the only person she could see was one of the part-time gardeners. She asked where Ivo was.

'He told me he was going to see Lisa. Her boys are ill. He said he wouldn't be long, he'd be back before I'd finished this job. But if he doesn't come soon I'll be idle. It doesn't matter to me if he's not here to give me more work. I'm paid by the day. Mind you, I can't blame him for lingering. She's a nice girl.'

'Thank you,' Fran interrupted quickly. 'When I find Ivo I'll tell him you'll soon be stuck for work.'

Fran walked so quickly to Lisa's cottage that she had little time to think. But crossing the lane which skirted the grounds at the back of The Court, she paused at Lisa's garden gate to regain her breath.

Going up the path, Fran's lips tightened slightly when she saw the large garden was reasonably well kept, no doubt Ivo's doing. Why should it matter to her if Ivo was helping Lisa? After all she wouldn't have much free time, what with looking after the two boys and working for Elizabeth.

Taking a deep breath, Fran was just about to knock softly on the door in case the boys were asleep, when their loud shouts and laughter told her they were very much awake and by the sound of it, not very ill. The noise seemed to be coming from upstairs and, standing back, Fran looked up at the window. Was Lisa up there, too? Surely not, for she would not have allowed such a rumpus. After thudding on the brass knocker several times, Fran walked around the cottage, peering into the windows, but there was no sign of either Lisa or Ivo. Reaching the back door and finding it unlocked, she went into the kitchen.

'Anyone at home?' she called loudly.

When there was no reply, she went to the foot of the stairs and was just going to call out again, when a rolled-up sheet caught her in the face. Ivo peered over the banister.

'Fran, I'm sorry, I didn't know you were there.'

Bundling up the orange-juice-soaked sheet, she replied with some feeling, 'With all that noise going on, I doubt you would have heard six elephants coming in.'

Ivo turned away to order the boys to be quiet. As a few suppressed giggles heralded silence, he came to the top of the stairs.

'Fran, I don't know why you've come, but as far as I'm concerned you're an angel in disguise.'

'I'm not sure how to take that,' she replied with relief for he seemed to have forgotten the incident in the attic. 'But where's Lisa? Is there anything I can do to help?'

'Lisa's gone shopping in Chepstow and rather rashly, I said I'd look after her two monsters. But as soon as their mother was out of sight, they decided to play me up and I'm afraid you see the consequence.'

Going up the stairs, Fran asked, 'Has the juice gone all over the place?'

'No, thank goodness,' Ivo said, leading the way into the boys' room. 'But I need to change bunk beds. There's chocolate over the other one.'

'Chocolate? They don't sound very ill to me.'

Going into the bedroom, Fran gasped at the mess.

'Have they done all of this since Lisa left?'

The two boys were now lying in their bunks on rumpled bedding, trying to look ill, but Ivo unceremoniously hauled them out.

'As they look like spotty dalmatians, perhaps I should tie them up in the garden.'

Hiding a smile, Fran suggested, 'How about letting them watch TV downstairs whilst we try to restore some order here?'

As they whooped with delight, Ivo hesitated.

'I don't know. Lisa said they had to stay in bed.'

'They can't stay in their beds, the state they're in and we'll get on a lot faster without them under our feet.'

'All right, you two, dressing-gowns on, then downstairs and switch on the telly. But no fooling about!'

As the boys pushed and jostled their way

out of the bedroom, Ivo went to fetch fresh sheets, whilst Fran stripped the bunks.

For a few minutes they worked without speaking, but all the time Fran was aware of Ivo's nearness. Several times he brushed against her and each time a shiver rippled through her. But he seemed unaware that he had touched her and she cursed her own awareness of him. Hurriedly, she finished the lower bunk and began tidying the room. She didn't realise she was rushing about, until Ivo put a restraining hand on her arm.

'Hey, what's the hurry?'

'I thought the boys should get back to bed as soon as possible,' she replied, glancing away from his teasing smile.

'Let's enjoy the peace and quiet while we can. Just look at you! You're as tense as a bow string. There's no need to be so anxious about the boys. They're not the weaklings Lisa thinks they are.'

'It's only natural she worries about them,' Fran mumbled.

Suddenly serious, Ivo moved in front of her, but she did not look up.

'Fran, I've been wanting to see you, but things got in the way.'

What things, Fran thought. What could have kept him away from The Court? Unless of course he had been regretting kissing her.

'Don't frown,' Ivo said softly, gently massaging her brow with finger tips slightly work roughened.

In the grip of chaotic thoughts, she wanted desperately to say something inconsequential.

'Your hands are rough,' she heard herself say with dismay, then to cover up this blunt observation, she added with a little laugh, 'But I don't suppose men wear gloves for gardening.'

But he had already snatched his hands away.

'Of course, you'll be used to the soft hands of office people like Geoff.'

Then before Fran could frame a reply, he left the room and ran down the stairs. She did not follow, but stood uncertainly. Should she go out through the front door, calling out a brief goodbye to the boys? Suppose though, Ivo continued to think she was longing for Geoff's touch. She smiled wryly, for to her surprise she could not recall the effect Geoff's physical presence had once exerted, not even his kisses. Wasn't this what she wanted, showing she had managed to erase Geoff from every fibre of her being and memory? But a small inner voice insisted unsettlingly that she could recall every time Ivo had touched her.

She was saved from more disturbing thoughts by the sound of a car and the boys' excited shouting as their mother came into the house. They had all gone into the kitchen so she couldn't hear any individual words only Ivo's deep tones and Lisa's light ones, interspersed by the boys' clamouring.

Slowly, Fran went down the stairs. There was no sneaking out now. She would have to say something to Lisa, explain her presence. Of course, she had come to ask Ivo about the gazebo! Doing just that would mask any awkwardness. But going into the kitchen, the words would not pass her dry lips, for the scene she saw was so intimate, so much like a family, that she felt an intruder.

'Fran, how nice to see you.' Lisa smiled, still standing by Ivo. 'I've just been hearing you've been helping to sort out the mess made by my two little devils.'

Fran knew her smile was tight, but only Ivo noticed as he looked at her over Lisa's head.

'I was glad to be able to help.'

To Fran, her words sounded horribly formal but they were drowned by the excited chatter of the boys as they rummaged in Lisa's carrier bag.

'I'm sorry I was out when you came. You should've phoned first.'

Fran nodded, but meeting Ivo's steady gaze, she wondered whether he always phoned before he came or was there always an open door for him? As he looked at her, she shifted from one foot to the other. It was as though he was trying to read her mind without giving away anything of himself.

'I'd better be going,' Fran said. Then taking a deep breath she said with the return of her usual briskness, 'Ivo, when you've the time,

67

there's trouble with the gazebo people. And I nearly forgot, the man in the kitchen garden asked me to tell you he's nearly finished, but that was some time ago.'

She knew her voice held a slight note of censure, but did not regret it. It was all very well Ivo and Lisa playing happy families, but there was work to be done.

CHAPTER EIGHT

Fran made no attempt to hide the fact that she was hurrying away from Lisa's and, taking a short cut through towering beech trees, she tried to concentrate on what to do about the gazebo. But the picture of Ivo, Lisa and the boys making such a happy family group kept intruding.

Then she realised with a shock, she and Geoff had never had a deep, intense closeness. Before she could consider this astonishing thought more, the sound of a furiously pedalled bike made her turn. She was just in time to see Ivo's bike hit a tree root, sending him somersaulting over the handlebars. All thoughts of Lisa and Ivo together vanished.

'Ivo, are you all right?' she shouted, running to where he lay.

'Fran, can you help get this bike off me? It seems somehow to have wrapped itself around me.'

Although she tried to be careful, Ivo exclaimed softly as the metal pressed into him.

'Sorry. I'll try to be as quick as possible,' she said, trying to twist the handlebars away from him, so he could slide out. 'There!'

Triumphantly she succeeded in up-ending the bike.

'Can you stand?'

He tried to rise, but with a gasp, fell back.

'Where does it hurt?' she asked anxiously, bending over him.

Already worrying thoughts were tumbling into her brain. Could Ivo manage to hobble home? If not, would he be all right while she got help?

'Fran, I think I . . .'

'What is it?' she asked, bending closer.

'I think I want to kiss you.'

Ivo's voice was as strong as the arms now holding her, and for a second she was too shocked to do or say anything. Then recent scenes of Ivo and Lisa flooded back, giving her the strength to pull away.

'What do you think you're doing?' she demanded angrily. 'You talk about Geoff, but you're as bad as him. No, you're much worse, for there weren't small, vulnerable children involved.'

'What do you mean?'

'Ask Lisa,' she hurled at him.

'I don't understand.'

69

'No, men like you never do. If you spent as much energy on your work, The Court gardens would be looking far better. After all that's what you're being paid for, not to fool around.'

'I wasn't fooling around.'

But Fran was already hurrying away. She was so intent on reaching the security of The Court, that it did not occur to her that Mrs Bowen might be in the kitchen.

'Whatever have you been doing?' the housekeeper exclaimed, seeing her dishevelled state as she came in. 'And you look so upset.'

'I've been to Lisa's and on the way back took a short cut through the beech wood.'

Then seeing Mrs Bowen wasn't satisfied with this, she hurriedly explained about Ivo falling off his bike and trying to help him.

'You haven't gone and left him, have you?'

Mrs Bowen's voice was heavy with disapproval.

'He seemed all right when I left,' Fran replied, edging towards the door into the house. 'You can always phone him to check.'

As if on cue, the phone rang, making them both jump.

'That could be Ivo now,' Mrs Bowen said, hurrying to answer it.

Fran hurried from the kitchen, not caring that this looked as though she was running away. Deciding she would feel better, more in control if she tidied herself up, she went to her room. A shower and fresh clothes would help

70

to regain her composure. She was soon standing under refreshing jets of water, eyes closed. If she could just wash away all memories of Geoff and Ivo. Somehow the two of them had become intertwined.

Then for the second time within a few minutes she heard the phone's urgent ringing, this time the extension in her room. Turning the water to a more fierce, noisy jet, she reached for the shampoo, anything to muffle the noise. It was still ringing when she turned off the water.

'All right! All right!' she said crossly. 'I'm coming.'

Hastily wrapping a towel around her hair, she used a large one to wrap around herself. Padding across to the phone, she sank down on the bed as she lifted the receiver. Assuming it was Mrs Bowen with news about Ivo, Fran spoke curtly.

'Yes? What is it?'

To her surprise it was not Mrs Bowen but her grandmother.

'Do you always answer the phone so aggressively?'

It seemed to Fran that Elizabeth had deliberately made her voice soft and low in contrast to her own harsh tones.

'Sorry, I was in the shower.'

'Trying to wash away whatever it is that's got into you?'

'I don't know what you mean,' Fran denied.

'I've been gardening, then in the wood.'

'Then in the wood you came upon Ivo.'

'How do you know that?' Fran interrupted. 'Oh, I know, Mrs Bowen told you. She certainly doesn't waste much time.'

'I asked her how things were and she told me. She says you seem to be falling out with Ivo at the drop of a hat.'

'We are not saints, so it's only natural we disagree sometimes.'

'I've never had cause to disagree with him. If we had a difference of opinion, we discussed it like two civilised people.'

'I don't know what Mrs Bowen has been saying to you,' Fran replied heatedly, 'but we have not been at each other's throats. It's just that we have a different sense of what's honourable.'

'Good gracious, Fran, you sound very Victorian talking about honour like that. What's got into you? You always used to find the good in everyone, even in that scoundrel, Geoff.'

'Perhaps it was he who made me realise I was very gullible. I'm not going to make the same mistake twice.'

'Are you saying you're attracted to Ivo, but are fighting it?' Elizabeth asked slowly.

'Certainly not! Ours is a purely working relationship.'

Fran's denial was so vehement that Elizabeth laughed.

'Methinks you protest too much.'

'Look, Gran, what were you actually phoning about?'

'Dear me, I nearly forgot. The doctor says my general health has improved so much that I can come home. Of course I will still be in plaster, but I can get up quite a good speed using elbow crutches.'

'Why, that's wonderful news,' Fran enthused, over the thought that with Elizabeth home, her sharp eyes would miss nothing.

This was underlined by the fact that although she couldn't see Fran, Elizabeth sensed all was not well.

'What is it, Fran? I won't interfere with your work, or Ivo's for that matter. You and he can continue as you have been doing.'

Fran smiled wryly. If she and Ivo continued in the up-and-down way which had become normal, Elizabeth would soon want to know why. And what could she say? That Ivo had been trying to flirt with her although he and Lisa obviously had a very close relationship? No! However difficult it might be, in future she would have to try to get along with Ivo, while keeping him at arms' length. Hopefully though, with eagle-eyed Elizabeth home, he would remember he was paid to see to the garden, not trying to be the local Casanova.

'Fran, are you still there?'

'Sorry, Gran, I was just wondering what we could do to make things easy for you here.'

'I'm not an invalid,' was the sharp reply. 'It's only this wretched leg that's not functioning properly, not my brain. Now, if you would ask Ivo if he'll be kind enough to fetch me tomorrow.'

'I'll come!' Fran interrupted.

'No, I want Ivo to bring his large estate car. With this plaster on my leg, I wouldn't be able to get into your small car, or mine.'

With a weary sigh Fran replaced the phone. Now she would have to contact Ivo and quickly. Why couldn't Elizabeth have done so herself?

A shiver reminding her she was cold, Fran dressed hurriedly in green cord pants and a matching thick sweater. The sooner she arranged things with Ivo, the better. As she impatiently tapped out his phone number, she rehearsed what she was going to say, making it brisk, businesslike, to the point. But his phone rang repeatedly, unanswered. Typical of the man, she fumed. Now she would have to leave a note in his cottage.

Although she could have easily walked to Ivo's, Fran went in her car wanting to get the unpleasant errand over and done with. It was only when she drew up outside the small, single-storey building, and saw Ivo's battered bike leaning drunkenly against the wall, that a wave of doubt hit her. Had he really been hurt after all?

Hastily getting out of the car, she took the

note she had written out of her pocket. She ran the few paces to the door and, not wanting to advertise her presence, pushed open the brass letter flap very carefully and slipped the note through, slowly easing her hand away. The flap was half closed when she heard footsteps crunching up the path behind her. As though caught in a reprehensible act, she let the flap drop with a clatter.

'If you had waited a minute, you could have given it to me,' Ivo said a little stiffly.

Fran did not turn immediately, but stood, eyes closed, to mask her alarm.

'Our paths must have crossed,' Ivo said. 'I've been down to The Court to find you, to apologise for my behaviour. It was inexcusable. I'm not surprised you don't want to face me.'

She turned slowly, knowing she had to look at him, otherwise it would seem as though she was refusing his apology. Even so, she wanted to end this very uncomfortable meeting, for she needed time to think, to adjust to the emotions Ivo kept stirring into life.

'I was just putting a note through your door about Elizabeth. She's coming home tomorrow and wonders if you could fetch her.'

'That's good news and of course I'll fetch her. But this does raise another problem. Before she comes home and senses something is wrong, you and I must try to bury our differences.'

'All will be well if you get on with your job

and I get on with mine.'

She knew she was on the defensive again. Why did Ivo have to make an issue out of nearly everything?

'Fran, look at me,' he ordered. 'I don't know why, but whenever we're together, tension seems to spring up between us. I know Geoff has a lot to answer for but . . .'

'There you go again, mentioning Geoff! If you had any tact at all, you would avoid his name. I want him firmly in the past, but you seem intent on seeing his name crops up as often as possible. If I didn't know any better, I'd say you knew him.'

'What on earth makes you say that?' he demanded sharply. 'I'm truly sorry mentioning him upsets you, but he does seem to be very near the surface of everything that happens between us.'

'Ivo, can't you get it into your head that what there was between Geoff and me has absolutely nothing to do with you? Can't we make a pact never to say his name again?'

'Of course!' he agreed.

They stood awkwardly, avoiding eye contact, wanting this confrontation to be over, but neither knowing how to make the first move. Then a frivolous thought had him smiling. Kissing was an excellent way of making amends! Before such an enticing thought could become an action that would spark off even more trouble, he held out his hand.

'Shaking hands seems a little formal, but let's see it as agreeing to make a fresh start,' he said instead.

Her swiftness in taking his hand pleasantly surprised Ivo, but her parting words did not.

'For Gran's sake, I agree. Keeping our relationship strictly business will solve a lot of problems.'

If Fran had not immediately walked away, she would have seen Ivo's look of uncertainty.

CHAPTER NINE

It was as though Elizabeth was returning from a long absence abroad, as Mrs Bowen alternated between muttering that The Court looked a mess, and scurrying around with cleaning materials. Nothing Fran could say would stop the housekeeper's whirlwind activity and so she sought refuge in the study, the door very firmly shut. She had plenty to keep her busy, including a phone call to the gazebo suppliers who had still not resolved the problem.

Early the following morning Ivo went to collect Elizabeth. Fran joined Mrs Bowen in the kitchen where the smell of home-baked scones filled the air.

When Ivo's estate car drew up as close to

the kitchen door as he could, both Mrs Bowen and Fran ran out to greet Elizabeth, but having found the journey more tiring than she thought it would be, Elizabeth waved them impatiently away, looking to Ivo to help her. Fran was unaware she was showing her disappointment until Mrs Bowen put a comforting arm around her waist.

'Come along, love, it's best Ivo helps her. He will be able to help her more than we can. You go into the drawing-room and see the fire is going well and that there's nothing in Elizabeth's way. It will be different moving around in the house to being in her room at the nursing home.'

Although Fran obeyed, she did so with a heavy heart. She should have been the one who brought Elizabeth in, not Ivo! Every way she turned, he seemed to be there.

Fran was just bending to poke the fire, when Elizabeth came in slowly on her elbow crutches.

'Why on earth have you lit the fire?' she asked shortly. 'It's not winter.'

Without looking up, Fran went to replace the poker but in her agitation, she let it fall with a clatter on to the stone hearth. Frayed by the car journey, Elizabeth muttered something under her breath. Easing Elizabeth into an armchair a little distance from the fire, Ivo tried to lighten the atmosphere.

'You'll soon feel better when you've had a

cup of tea and a scone.'

'Stop talking to me as though I was a doddering old fool,' Elizabeth snapped, waving Ivo away. 'It's my leg that's the problem, not my brain.'

Fran had not meant to look at Ivo, but as she went towards Elizabeth, she caught his sympathetic half smile. But instead of cheering her, she felt another twist of annoyance.

'We can manage now, thank you,' she said briskly. 'We mustn't keep you from your work.'

'There's no need to talk to Ivo like that,' Elizabeth said, when he'd gone.

Having settled comfortably into the chair, her leg up on a stool, she was now wearily calm.

'I'd hoped you were on better terms with him. He's first class at his job.'

'No doubt he is, but he's not family.'

She knew she sounded petty, childish even, but she wasn't used to Elizabeth putting anyone before her.

'Fran, I've enough on my plate with this wretched leg, without you taking up against him.'

'I haven't taken up against him at all,' she protested, then seeing how tired Elizabeth looked, she added with a half-apologetic shrug, 'I suppose if I was honest, I'd confess that it will take me some time to get over Geoff's treachery.'

'That's a poor excuse for your behaviour. I

would not have expected that from you. Do you really mean that whatever hurt we've had, it gives us the right to lash out at the next unsuspecting person who just happens along?'

Avoiding her grandmother's stern look, Fran shook her head. Elizabeth's words had struck home.

'Well, then, I don't want to hear another word against Ivo.'

It wasn't only Elizabeth who set Fran trying to see Ivo in a different light, for next day, looking at the accounts on the computer, she saw he was being paid far less than she imagined an expert would demand. For a couple of minutes she sat staring at the screen, wondering if the figures were correct. Although Lisa's children were now better, she wasn't at The Court that day so Fran couldn't ask her about the puzzling payments to Ivo. So instead she decided to talk to her grandmother who was feeling much better after a good night's sleep in her own bed.

'Gran,' Fran began, going into the drawing-room, 'did Ivo sign a contract or something before he started?'

'Not Ivo again.' Elizabeth sighed. 'Why do you ask about a contract? Why are you checking up on him?'

'I'm not checking up on him at all! It's just that I've been looking at the accounts and noticed how small the payments to him have been. Has there been some mistake?'

'I'm delighted that for once you seem to have Ivo's best interests at heart. I don't suppose there's any harm in you knowing that Ivo offered to restore the gardens for a comparatively small amount because he knew I really could not afford his usual fee. Satisfied? He says that no doubt there will be magazine articles about The Court and this will give him good publicity.'

That afternoon Fran had to go into Bristol to discuss a problem with the printers who were doing the coloured guide books for The Court. Although Fran wasn't eager to return to the city, she tried to tell herself that the chances of meeting either Geoff or Anita were slender.

The area around the printers was new to her and it took her some time to find the right street and longer still to find a parking space. When she finally pushed open the door of the printers, her one thought was to get the problem sorted as quickly as possible and return to the peacefulness of The Court. Thirty minutes later, it was with a sigh of relief she headed back to her car, key in hand, ready for a quick getaway from Bristol's noisy bustle.

She was just opening the car door when someone shouted her name. An automatic reaction had her turning before she realised the caller's identity.

'Fran, how are you? You're looking as beautiful as ever.'

Geoff's loud greeting had passersby smiling, but not Fran. Wooden-faced, she hurriedly got into the car but as she tried to slam the door shut, Geoff ran up and grabbed it.

'Let go,' she ordered. 'If you don't, I'll just drive away.'

'And the door will hit either another car or pedestrian, and you'll be charged with careless driving.'

'I've absolutely nothing to say to you,' she snapped.

'But I've something to say to you. It's all over with Anita. If you hadn't dashed away before I could explain . . .'

'Explain? That clinch you were in with her needed no explanation, and as for Anita, she's had a lucky escape.'

Making no attempt to release the car door, Geoff continued silkily.

'I hear you're holed up at The Court. Isn't it time you let go of your grandmother's apron string and came back into the real world?'

'For your information I did not run away to Gran. She broke her leg and needed help.'

For the first time, Geoff looked a little uncomfortable and lifted his head slightly to avoid Fran's look of loathing. Seeing this, she put both hands on the door handle and heaved it shut. Then hurriedly pushing down the door lock, she turned on the ignition and as though sensing her urgency, the engine sprang into life. Pulling away from the pavement, she glanced into her rear-view mirror and smiled as she saw Geoff standing open-mouthed. Almost immediately he was lost in the crowd.

CHAPTER TEN

'Fran, I've got to go away for two or three days,' Ivo began as he came into the study carrying another pot of flowers, but this time of crimson polyanthus.

'Is the plant a sweetener because you want me to do something for you whilst you're not here?' Fran asked with a smile as she looked up from the computer screen.

She didn't know if it was Elizabeth's presence, but a kind of peace seemed to have enveloped Fran, despite having recently seen Geoff. So when she and Ivo had met or talked over the phone, these contacts were agreeable, friendly.

'Now would I stoop to a bribe?' Ivo asked, replacing the fading hyacinths with the polyanthus. 'There, that's better. I like white flowers but the trouble is they soon lose their perfection.'

'Will you throw the bulbs away?'

'No, I'll use them again next year, but the flowers might not be so big.'

'That doesn't matter to me, as long as they have that lovely perfume.'

'So you're going to stay on then?'

She looked away, staring at the computer screen as though it could show her the future. She hadn't even told Elizabeth about the unexpected meeting with Geoff, nor how this had finally decided her not to go back to Bristol. It might be a large city and even though the chance of bumping into him again might be small, she didn't want to take the risk. That part of her life was over with. But the future?

'You're miles away,' Ivo said softly.

Glancing up, she was wondering whether to tell him about her resolve not to return to Bristol, when something in his expression stopped her. It was as though her answer was really important in some way, and feeling a prickle of apprehension, she did not reply.

She wasn't aware she was frowning until he asked gently, 'What is it, Fran? You're sitting there with your mouth open like a startled goldfish.'

'I was just going to ask where you were off to, but it sounds nosey.'

'I don't see why. It's no big secret. I designed a roof garden for a client in London and he's not happy with some of the planting. It seems his latest girlfriend doesn't like the colour scheme. At the outset, I did tell Elizabeth that occasionally I would need to take a few days away from here.'

'Of course.' Fran managed to smile. 'You're

due quite a lot of time off for you work through every week-end.'

Well, nearly every week-end, she thought, for he often spent time with Lisa and her two sons. She knew this for a fact because Lisa seemed to make a point of telling Fran every time Ivo went to her house.

Then, feeling guilty because of this uncharitable thought, she added hastily, 'it must be a large roof if it's going to take so much time.'

'I've other matters to see to in London.'

He left so abruptly that Fran stared after him in surprise. Why had her comment precipitated such a reaction? Had he a relationship which he wanted to keep secret? If so, it was a very odd one, for he hadn't had any visitors, and from his mail, all of which came to The Court, she had noticed that nearly all of it looked to do with his work. But could this lack of visitors and letters be the result of a lovers' tiff?

With a shrug, she turned back to her work. Ivo's personal affairs were nothing to do with her, as long as he did his work properly at The Court.

*   *   *

'You're lost in thought. I hope you're not regretting finishing with Geoff.'

For the second time that day, Fran's

85

absentmindedness was commented upon, only this time by her grandmother. Although it was mild, the afternoon was overcast and Elizabeth had asked Fran to light the drawing-room fire to lift the gloom. Elizabeth was in her usual armchair, her leg up on a stool, Fran sitting on the floor by the hearth gazing at the flames licking the logs.

'Is everything OK?' Elizabeth asked. 'Is it the gazebo company again?'

Fran swiftly assured her that the new gazebo would be arriving within a few days. But knowing that if she didn't say anything more, Elizabeth would keep on probing, she got to her feet and wandered over to the window.

'I was just wondering about Ivo. I think he's leaving to drive to London tonight and it looks as though it might be misty.'

'I wouldn't worry. Ivo will be careful. He's not one to take risks, but I'm delighted you've got over your initial distrust of him. Ivo isn't the slightest bit like that scoundrel, Geoff.'

Fran had her back to the room so Elizabeth only saw her nod. What she could not see was her granddaughter's uncertain frown as she realised that she was indeed worrying about Ivo. Fran left shortly after that, for Elizabeth had apologetically told her that nothing much had been done about seeking publicity for The Court. It was already late for some organisations, but familiar with the ins and outs of publicity from her work with the

86

advertising agency, Fran hurried away to contact newspapers and tourist organisations.

Before she began, she decided to jog around the grounds, hoping that doing so would banish thoughts and questions about Ivo which continued to sneak up on her. Changing into a tracksuit, she set out towards the wood, but it was so dank there she decided to return by cutting across to the drive. By now the mist had thickened to a drizzle and disliking its clammy feel, she pulled up the hood of her top.

She didn't hear Ivo's car approach from behind until it was level with her and he had braked suddenly.

'Fran, what on earth are you doing out in this?' he asked sharply, winding down his window. 'Don't you know better than to wear dark clothing when there are cars about? Get in. I'll take you back to the house.'

'It's not far.'

'I said get in!' and to reinforce his order, he leaned across to open the passenger door.

Aware for the first time of the penetrating damp, Fran nodded her thanks, but she had to wait a few seconds whilst Ivo hurriedly picked up a couple of folders from the seat. Then as he turned to put them on the back seat, the cover of one of them flipped open and before he hastily closed it, Fran thought she saw several sheets of paper which did not have the pristine look of newness. She wasn't sure, but was the top page a faded sketch of a garden?

'I'm sorry,' she mumbled, getting into the car. 'I didn't think. When I set out, I intended keeping to the wood but it was so unpleasant there.'

'And I'm sorry, too. That makes two of us!'

Now it was Ivo's turn to apologise as he put the car into gear.

'I shouldn't have shouted at you like that, but if I'd been driving fast, I could have knocked you down.'

Although the ensuing silence only lasted a few seconds, it seemed to Fran to stretch into an uncomfortable length and she sought to break it by saying the first thing that came into her head.

'If you're not in a hurry, when we reach the house, I'll find you a large envelope for those files. You don't want the papers falling out from them.'

'No, there's no need. My briefcase is on the back seat. I nearly forgot them and left the engine running whilst I went back into the house.'

Fran did not have the chance to say anything more for Ivo had drawn up outside The Court.

'Thanks for the lift,' she began as he hurriedly leaned over to the back seat to push the folders under the briefcase.

Then turning back, he suddenly put his arm around her. Before she could say anything, he had kissed her quickly.

' 'Bye, Fran.'

He moved away, hands on the gear lever and steering wheel, impatient to be on his way. Now out of the car, she stood back.

He didn't hear her automatically spoken, 'Take care!'

As the car's rear lights disappeared around a bend, Fran's hand went to touch her lips. His kiss had been so light and swift that she wondered if she had imagined it. But, no, he had put his arm around her. Going slowly back into the house, ignoring the fact that she was damp, she forced herself to concentrate on writing eye-catching publicity pieces about The Court opening to the public. But every now and again, her fingers went to her lips and aware of this, she hastily told herself not to be so silly. It had only been an absentminded kiss, the sort given when leaving.

That night, waking in a panic which had sent her heart racing, Fran lay rigid, trying to remember if she'd had a nightmare. But then she remembered. Ivo! She had been dreaming vividly that he had kissed her, then he had turned into Geoff who laughingly told her that a kiss would stop her revealing his evil plans which were contained in folders.

Taking several deep breaths, she tried to find reasons for the nightmare. Geoff, well, it might take some time for him to disappear entirely from her subconscious. But the garden plans—now there was something more concrete. Getting up to straighten the rumpled sheet and duvet, she firmly resolved to try to find out about them before Ivo returned.

In the reassuring light of day, Fran tried to smile as she recalled the nightmare, but try as she might, she couldn't rid herself of the feeling of unease about Ivo's seeming haste in tucking away those old pages. If only she could talk to someone about it, even if they told her she was being silly. She couldn't say anything to Elizabeth for she would no doubt accuse her of always thinking the worst of Ivo. Mrs Bowen, too, seemed to think Ivo was a saint! There was one person who didn't accuse her of being anti-Ivo—Lisa!

After breakfast, she waited for Lisa in her office.

'My goodness, you're an early bird,' Lisa exclaimed, hooking her shoulder bag over the back of her chair. 'There's nothing wrong, is there?'

'Nothing's wrong. I was just a little curious about something . . . well, worried, I suppose. I've found out that Ivo's fee for the gardens isn't nearly enough. I do feel a little guilty, as though we're taking advantage of him.'

'I don't see why you're talking to me. Surely it's Elizabeth you should be asking,' Lisa said absently, switching on her computer.

'No, I don't want to do that,' Fran heard herself lying easily. 'Besides not wanting to

90

worry her, I don't want her thinking that I feel she's not paying Ivo enough,' she finished with an awkward little laugh.

'I still don't see how I can help.'

Fran wasn't going to let the subject drop.

'I know he isn't paying any rent and he gets some of his meals here, but with freelance work, you've got to make enough to tide you over lean times.'

'Oh, I see what you mean, but there's no need to worry. Ivo has several irons in the fire. He's not just dependent on what Elizabeth is paying him.'

'Thanks, that's put my mind at rest,' Fran said as she left.

But once outside the office, she leaned her back against the closed door. In reality, her mind was far from being at rest! Was Ivo using the old garden notes and plans to write and sell articles? If so, why had he been so secretive about it? Elizabeth would have been more than willing for him to make use of them. Or was he writing a book, perhaps about old gardens and their restoration? His work at The Court would make very interesting reading, especially if backed up by old garden plans.

Yet again he looked like a man who wasn't being open, above board.

CHAPTER ELEVEN

Back in the study, Fran was still trying to digest what Lisa had told her about Ivo, when a grim-faced Mrs Bowen came in, leaving the door ajar as though she was being watchful.

'There's someone to see you,' she announced. 'He's in the kitchen. I would rather he wasn't there under my feet, but in the circumstances I guess you wouldn't want your grandmother seeing him.'

'Seeing whom?' Fran asked.

'That good-for-nothing from Bristol.'

'Do you mean Geoff?'

When Mrs Bowen nodded, Fran got up hastily, muttering under her breath, 'What can he want? Couldn't you have said I was out?'

'No, I could not!'

Geoff had come down the corridor so quietly that neither Fran nor Mrs Bowen knew he was there until he entered the room.

'Fran, I'm ashamed of you, asking Mrs Bowen to lie.'

Before Fran could reply, Mrs Bowen turned to face him.

'Perhaps that's a measure of her dislike of you. If you hadn't caught me unawares I wouldn't have had you in the house. But not for you the polite knock and waiting to be asked in. You marched straight into my kitchen as though you owned it.'

'I never used to knock before.'

'Then, you hadn't behaved so wickedly to Fran.'

With one last glare at Geoff as she swept past him, Mrs Bowen went, but she left the door wide open. She was going to remain in earshot just in case there was trouble. A bit of her wished Ivo hadn't gone to London.

With lazy ease Geoff perched on the corner of the desk, turning down the corner of his mouth in mock innocence that at one time would have had Fran laughing, but not any more.

'To hear that old biddy, you'd think I had robbed a bank,' he joked.

'That old biddy is called Mrs Bowen,' Fran snapped.

Not wanting to rile her, Geoff got off the desk but he was smiling as though they were playing a game and he knew all the moves. This did not intimidate Fran for suddenly she felt totally in control. At last she was able to look at him dispassionately.

'What do you want?' she snapped, indicating her hardness of heart.

'Can't a bloke make a social call?' he asked.

'How can you think even for a second that after all that has happened, you could possibly make a social call here?' she asked sarcastically.

'All right, Fran, I'll come straight to the

point.'

But with an old trick of his, he paused for effect. She smiled, not to encourage him but because she was actually enjoying herself. For the first time since she had known him, she sensed she had the upper hand.

Encouraged by her smile, he crossed to the door which he shut, saying loudly, 'We don't want any eavesdroppers, do we?'

Then sitting down on a chair, legs crossed, hands behind his head, he looked up at Fran.

'Why don't you sit down? Or are you ready to run to Mrs Bowen?'

'I'm standing because I want you out of this room, this house.'

Ignoring her obvious desire for him to leave, Geoff spoke as though there was no animosity between them.

'We've talked many times about setting up our own advertising agency.'

'Daydreamed, not talked,' Fran corrected firmly.

'Have it your own way, but call it what you like, you must agree we made a good team when we worked together. I've got contacts.'

'If you've got contacts, what's stopping you setting up in business? I'm sure Anita would be only too happy to work for you.'

'I've told you, we're finished. She made all the running.'

'From what I saw, you were easily caught. Now, please go, I've work to do, even if you

94

haven't.'

Marching past him, she opened the door wide, but Geoff was not willing to be so easily dismissed.

'Fran, sweetheart,' he said huskily, rising to put his hands on her shoulders. 'Let's be adult about this. I want to be my own boss and you've no job.'

'You could have fooled me,' she said, looking pointedly at her IN-tray. 'I don't need you, or another job.'

'I refuse to believe you're happy.'

He stopped, a sound he could not identify making him frown. Fran, though, knew it was Elizabeth's crutches, and not wanting her grandmother to be involved with Geoff, she spoke quickly.

'Are you to go, or shall I get one of the gardeners to throw you out?'

'You mean that decrepit, old man who comes in occasionally? Don't make me laugh! He can hardly hold a hoe, let alone . . .'

'If you need physical persuasion to help you on your way, then I can provide it,' Elizabeth said softly from behind him.

Turning and seeing she had lifted one of her crutches a few inches off the ground, Geoff exclaimed, 'Elizabeth! I didn't know you were here.'

'Why not? It is my house and I can't remember inviting you in.'

Always quick to recover, Geoff tried a

winning smile as he replied, 'I just dropped in to see how Fran was. But I'm sorry you've been in the wars.'

'More like you're sorry that I'm here! I always thought you had a thick skin, so how many times do you have to be told to go, before it sinks in?'

Recognising that Fran and Elizabeth together were a strong alliance, without another word, he marched down the corridor, banging doors as he passed through the kitchen on his way out.

'Thanks, Gran, for coming to my rescue,' Fran said a little shakily. 'But I could have managed on my own.'

'You might have, but you see, I'm not totally convinced you are entirely resistant to that man's persuasive ways.'

As Fran opened her mouth to voice a hot denial, Elizabeth continued.

'When you were so wary with Ivo, I put it down to once bitten, twice shy, but now I'm not so sure. It could just be that a bit of you is still hankering after Geoff but deep down you know it's folly, so you lash out at Ivo.'

'You make me sound like some silly, young girl. I've told you, I've finished with Geoff, and as for taking it out on Ivo, that's plain daft. He doesn't come into the equation at all. I know at times I've been a little disagreeable with him, but you must admit it's only natural that I should be wary of men for a while.'

'As long as it doesn't become a habit,' Elizabeth said, turning to go slowly back to the drawing-room.

Suddenly feeling very tired, empty, Fran slipped out of the front door. She needed to get away, to sit and think in the quiet solitude of the garden. Although she hated to admit it, perhaps Geoff had been right about one thing—she wasn't really happy at The Court. It had been a convenient refuge to get away from him, but perhaps she needed to put a greater distance between them, go far enough away so he would never be able to find her.

That evening, as Elizabeth thankfully let Fran help her to undress and get into bed, she became aware that her granddaughter was unusually preoccupied. But she didn't say anything until Fran had finished straightening the duvet and was picking up Elizabeth's discarded clothes.

'Fran, dear, you've been quiet ever since Geoff left and I'm wondering if he said something to upset you. Want to tell me about it, if I promise not to accuse you of still having a soft spot for him?'

Elizabeth had stretched out her hand as though in a gesture of peace and going slowly to the bed, Fran sat down. As Elizabeth gave her hand a squeeze, Fran looked up. Elizabeth looked so tired, vulnerable, perhaps now was not a good time to voice her half-formed decision.

'Come on, Frances, out with it!' Elizabeth ordered.

Fran smiled. Perhaps her grandmother was stronger than she looked.

'I've been thinking,' she began slowly.

'That much is obvious. But whatever it was about, it doesn't seem to have filled you with joy.'

Then pulling herself farther into the middle of the double bed, Elizabeth patted the space by her side.

'Come and put your feet up by me, like you used to do when you were a little girl. You liked me to tell you stories, but you're too big for that now.'

Fran obeyed, but she neither looked at her grandmother nor spoke.

'Fran, tell me I'm wrong, that you haven't decided to go back to that scoundrel.'

'I'm not that silly!' Fran said vehemently.

Then she paused for so long that Elizabeth leaned forward awkwardly to put a comforting arm round her. At this old reassuring touch, Fran's words came tumbling out.

'I think I should leave here, make a fresh start somewhere far away. Everything's nearly ready now for the opening of the house. There's nothing left Lisa can't deal with.'

'I never thought you one to run away,' Elizabeth said slowly.

Stung by her grandmother's disappointed tone, Fran denied hotly, 'I'm not running away. I just think it's time I moved on.'

'I do realise that once I'm on my feet there will not be enough for you to do here, but why the need to go far away? Despite what you said earlier, has Geoff still got a hold on you? Come on, Frances, out with it!'

There it was again, her grandmother's use of her proper name, a sure sign she would brook no nonsense.

'I need a fresh start. Of course I like it here at The Court with you, but I need a fresh challenge, a new job.'

Fran felt rather than saw Elizabeth nod her head in agreement and this gave her the courage to look directly at her.

'You do see, don't you?'

Her question was edged with a plea for understanding.

'Yes, I do. But before you pack your bags and race off, can I ask you a favour? Will you stay here just a little longer? I know there isn't much left to do about the house opening, but I could do with a little company, just until I get back into my stride,' she said, patting her plastered leg.

'Of course, I'll stay! I wasn't planning on going right away.'

They both knew this last sentence wasn't the truth, but Elizabeth let it pass. She had got what she wanted—Fran staying at The Court.

'I'm glad that's settled,' she said, leaning back on the pile of pillows. 'But suddenly I'm very tired. It's been quite a hectic day and I need to think of a challenge which will keep you happy here.'

CHAPTER TWELVE

During the next few days Elizabeth seemed determined to keep Fran by her side. At first Fran thought it was because her grandmother was still wondering if she would leave The Court precipitately, but didn't want to raise the subject in case it led back to Geoff. But the one person whom Elizabeth seemed to bring into the conversation at the slightest opportunity was Ivo. If she thought Geoff the biggest rogue in the world, then she seemed to consider Ivo in an entirely different light.

Walking very slowly around the garden one glorious afternoon, Fran was only half listening to Elizabeth extolling Ivo's gardening skills. The gardens and grounds were indeed looking good but why did Elizabeth have to go on so? Why couldn't her grandmother understand that all men were a taboo subject?

Fran wasn't aware she had been sighing until Elizabeth commented sharply, 'I thought you were interested in the restoration of the gardens but I seem to be boring you.'

'Of course I'm interested. Things look lovely.'

'Things? Is that the best you can do? To hear you, anyone would think you didn't know a peony from a snowdrop. Even when you were a child, you knew the name of flowers and shrubs from going around the garden with your grandfather. Which reminds me, how is the herb garden progressing? I know I shouldn't have let it go like I did, but what with one thing and another it always seemed to be at the end of the lists of jobs to be tackled. You will finish it for me, before you go? Your grandfather would be pleased to know you had rescued it and it will remind me of you both.'

Feeling guilty that she hadn't recently worked much in the herb garden, Fran was a little flustered as she replied.

'Good heavens, Gran, I won't be going to the end of the world. I know I haven't come here much recently, but that won't happen again, I promise.'

'Hush, dear!' Elizabeth ordered, head on one side as she listened intently. 'I think I can hear Ivo's car. He'll be tired after being in London and the drive back, so run and ask him to dinner this evening.'

'Dinner? That sounds very grand. Is it a special occasion? If I'd known, I would have brought my tiara with me.'

Fran forced herself to sound light-hearted so Elizabeth couldn't once again accuse her of being anti-Ivo.

Once out of sight, Fran walked slowly,

pensively. If she hurried, Ivo might think she was trying to make more of that snatched kiss. Involuntarily her fingers went to her lips as though touching them would recall that so-brief contact. She sighed. Life was so complicated. She hadn't wanted any romantic entanglement after Geoff, well, not for a long time, not until the pain of his treachery had dulled and she could look at men without a small voice reminding her they could be philanderers.

'Hi, Fran. Nice to see you!'

She had no need to go in search of Ivo for he was coming towards her, still in his smart, city clothes. He had discarded the suit jacket and tie, but the expert cut of the trousers emphasised his trim waist and long legs. His cream, short-sleeved shirt set off the year-round tan he had from being outside in all weathers. Then, realising she had not returned his greeting, just stared at him, she spoke hurriedly, gabbling.

'Did everything go well? Was London crowded? I always feel sorry for people in towns when the weather is glorious.'

He stopped right in front of her so she had no option but to look up at him a little apprehensively. What would she see in those brown eyes? Teasing mockery at the remembrance of that kiss? For a second their eyes met and she was surprised to see nothing but happiness in his. He, though, saw a shadow of remembered hurt which made his jaw tighten. If he ever saw Geoff . . .

'Everything been all right whilst I've been away?' he asked and although he was still smiling, Fran sensed this was no casual enquiry.

'Fine! Everything's been just fine,' she replied with a certainty which told him very clearly this was not so, but now was not the time to probe.

'Gran wants you to come to dinner tonight,' she said, turning so now she was by his side and he could not see her face clearly, nor her his.

'Dinner! What's the occasion?' he demanded.

Could it be that the meal was a farewell for Fran?

'It's just one of Gran's whims. Occasionally she likes to dress up and give Mrs Bowen the excuse to excel herself in the kitchen. I think it takes her back to when things were far more formal here.'

'I don't want to let the side down but I've nothing very formal here in the way of clothes.'

'That doesn't matter, neither have I. I left my party frocks in Bristol.'

'You'd look great even in a sack!'

'Tied up in one?' she asked, then inwardly cringed.

Would Ivo think she was flirting?

'I'm sure one of those very modern dress

designers could turn out something stunning.'

Taking her hands, he turned to face her.

'You'd look like a wood nymph.'

Then seeing her lips part to reply, he bent to kiss them briefly.

'Fran, there's no need to look so afraid of a little flirting. It can be harmless, something to put a spring in your step, a gleam in your eye. The time to be careful is when things change, become serious, wanting commitment.'

She nodded, swallowing hard.

'I've got out of practice, of a light-hearted friendship that is.'

He seemed to want to say more, but breaking free of his grasp, Fran began to walk back to The Court.

'See you tonight then,' she called over her shoulder with what she hoped was just the right amount of casualness.

Although still wishing Elizabeth hadn't asked Ivo to dinner, Fran wanted to look her best. Hurrying to her room, she tried all sorts of combinations with the casual clothes she had with her. Her denim jeans looked too workaday, the cords too heavy. Of course there was the denim skirt, but putting it on and twirling in front of the mirror, she decided it made her look dumpy.

Eventually realising that sitting at the table it was only her top which would be visible, she opted for navy-blue cords and a short blouse in a soft orange. For everyday, she used very little make-up, but that evening she decided to concentrate on her eyes, using shadow and mascara to accentuate their colour. Then, just as she heard Elizabeth's door open, Fran reached for her glossy orange lipstick. If Ivo saw this highlighting of her lips as an invitation then . . .

'Fran, are you ready? Can you come and pick up my handkerchief? I shall be glad when I'm out of this wretched plaster and can bend down again.'

Hurrying out of her room to where her grandmother was standing near the top of the stairs, Fran was able to glance down into the hall. Ivo was already there, looking up at them both with a wide smile. Then he turned away, for he knew Elizabeth would not like him watching her slow descent. Going over to a little antique table, he seemed to be preoccupied with the flower arrangement Fran had done.

Then as Elizabeth and Fran reached the hall, he came towards them, holding out two small sprays of flowers.

'I thought that as tonight was a special occasion, flowers would be nice for you both.'

First he went to Elizabeth, where, after seeing her nod of acceptance, he pinned two intertwined white rose buds on the bodice of her velvet dress.

'How considerate of you,' Elizabeth murmured. 'I didn't know your considerable

105

skills also included making corsages.'

'I'm interested in anything to do with flowers and plants,' he replied, turning to Fran.

She hadn't moved from the bottom of the stairs, but when he came towards her and aware Elizabeth was watching, Fran moved forwards. Her eyes were fixed on the dainty strands of early-flowering honeysuckle in his hand. She gulped, trying to force down the apprehension tightening her throat. Would he fasten the flowers on her as he had done for Elizabeth? Should she take the honeysuckle from him? But then he was speaking, holding out the sweet-smelling honeysuckle.

'From what you said earlier about not having a party frock, I thought you might like flowers that weren't so formal.'

Tension making it hard to move her lips in a smile, she took the proffered flowers, bending her head to smell their fragrance.

'They're just right,' she said, making no attempt to pin them on, for with his eyes on her, she knew she would fumble.

She was saved by Elizabeth saying that if they stood about much longer they would be in Mrs Bowen's bad books. Touching Fran's hand swiftly, Ivo went to Elizabeth, making her laugh with some remark about not being able to offer his arm because of her crutches. This gave Fran the opportunity to watch him as he crossed the hall to the small, intimate dining-room. Ivo might not have had any formal clothes with him, but dressed in elegant black trousers and shirt, Fran quickly stifled the thought that he looked stunning.

Hurriedly she turned her attention to the honeysuckle, pinning it on her shirt blouse as she chided herself for reacting so easily to the sight of an attractive man. If she didn't watch out, she would make a fool of herself! She mustn't make the mistake of being swayed by a man's physical appearance, especially so soon after Geoff. But over the meal she would have to be careful, making just the right amount of conversation so as not to give Elizabeth the opportunity to comment later on her behaviour.

They had hardly sat down at the highly-polished, circular table, when Mrs Bowen came hurrying in with the cordless phone.

'It's for you,' she announced, handing it to Ivo. 'I hope it won't take long. Everything is ready to serve.'

With an apologetic smile to Elizabeth and Fran, Ivo took the phone, his brusque, 'Yes?' clearly indicating he was not happy at being contacted at such a time. He listened for a few seconds before interrupting the caller.

'Couldn't you get someone else? It's most inconvenient right now.'

The caller seemed to be talking with some urgency, despite Ivo repeating that he would come later.

'What's wrong?' Elizabeth demanded.

Not bothering to cover the phone, Ivo's face and voice were bleak.

'It seems Lisa's drains are blocked.'

'Can't it wait until morning when I can get a plumber to her?' Elizabeth asked, obviously annoyed.

Lisa must have heard this, for listening to her again, Ivo replied wearily, 'I'm sure the boys won't come to any harm. They're in bed, aren't they?'

He listened again, then with a deep sigh of resignation handed the phone back to Mrs Bowen.

'Sorry, I'd better go and calm her down. I won't be long.'

He glanced at Fran, but she was intent on studying the leather place mat. As he hastily left, Elizabeth voiced Fran's thoughts.

'Lisa obviously knew Ivo was here. I wonder if she also knew we had invited him to dinner.'

CHAPTER THIRTEEN

Ivo did not return that evening. Gripped by different emotions, Elizabeth and Fran ate automatically whilst Mrs Bowen showed her annoyance by clattering dishes and plates. Fran tried to fight off the feeling of disappointment, but with little success. This followed her to bed where she spent a restless night tossing and turning.

Dawn seemed to be a long time coming, but when it did, she threw back the duvet and swung her legs to the floor. She was not going to let last night's episode get to her!

In her haste to get out into the refreshing air of a new day, she took twice as long to struggle into her tracksuit and trainers, but after that, her urge to put the past behind her gave her speed. Leaving quietly by the back door, Fran sped easily across the gardens before plunging into the beech wood. Reaching the rickety fence which indicated the boundary of The Court's land, she vaulted over it and into the huge expanse of the Forest of Dean.

Reaching a clearing where trees had been felled, she had a clear view down into the narrow valley where Tintern village and its abbey sheltered. Her eyes were drawn to the majestic grey stone ruins of the abbey and its rapidly filling carpark. What time was it? Hastily she pushed up her sleeve, then sighed as she remembered she had not put on her watch. But she did not need it to tell her that it was way past the time she normally had breakfast.

If Gran sent Mrs Bowen to look for her in her bedroom, the housekeeper might possibly see that her jogging clothes had gone. On the other hand . . . With a surge of annoyance at

109

her own thoughtlessness, Fran turned to retrace her steps hurriedly. The last thing she wanted was to cause Elizabeth any worry.

Reaching the grounds of The Court, she decided the quickest way to the house was down the back drive, and with luck she would be able to shower and gather her thoughts before she saw Mrs Bowen or Elizabeth. Under the cooling spray of the shower, guilt niggled at her. She should have told Elizabeth she was back. But on the other hand, when she did see her grandmother, she wanted to be cool, calm, ready to face no doubt probing questions. Ten minutes later, she was halfway down the stairs when she heard Elizabeth's raised voice in the drawing-room.

Was she berating Ivo for his behaviour the previous evening? But pausing to listen, it was not Ivo's deep tones she could hear, but a tearful Lisa. Peering over the banister, she saw Ivo striding to the drawing-room. Hastily she shrank back, but he was oblivious to all else, except Elizabeth's angry words and Lisa's muffled tears.

As he thrust open the door, she heard him ask, 'What's going on?'

Ivo did not bother to close the door and so Fran was able to hear most of what was said. It appeared Elizabeth had summoned Lisa to ask icily why Ivo's presence had been so urgently needed and what had prevented him returning to The Court? Lisa then poured out a long and tangled tale of woe which Elizabeth's probing questions could not stop.

Trying hard to remember her resolve not to be cynical, Fran then heard Ivo agree the drains had needed attention but whether immediately or not, he had refused to say. He did admit though that he should have phoned The Court to say he would not be returning. After several seconds' reflection, broken only by Lisa's nose blowing, Elizabeth accepted Ivo's apology, then impatiently waved them both away.

Waiting until Lisa had fled and Ivo had left by the front door, Fran wondered whether to go to Elizabeth or seek the sanctuary of the study. Her mind was made up for her by Mrs Bowen, who, crossing the hall, glanced up the stairs and, seeing Fran, told her briefly Elizabeth was best left alone to calm down.

Although she had been able to systematically sort various snippets into what she thought was a reasonable account of events, Fran balked at trying to fathom out what exactly was behind Lisa's actions, and Ivo's. So leaving the study she went into the herb garden. There, hard work would give her thoughts time to crystallise. But this was not to be, for a few minutes later just as she was driving the garden fork into the soil, she became aware of Ivo standing behind her.

'Is that me, Lisa, your grandmother, or the world you're attacking there?' he asked evenly.

Leaning on the fork handle, Fran did not turn to face him until she had gathered her wits. Then lifting the fork to prod a clod of soil, she spoke slowly, carefully.

'Quite a lot has happened during the last ten hours or so and I want to distance myself from it.'

'From the way you're avoiding looking at me, I guess you still haven't completely achieved your objective.'

Throwing down the fork, she turned swiftly to confront him.

'There's no problem in putting distance between you and me, because it's there already. You just work here.'

'Working here doesn't mean there's no involvement with the other people around me.'

When he paused, Fran fought back the urge to rush in. Perhaps he would say something about Lisa, though she told herself the only reason this would be of interest to her was because of working closely with the secretary.

'Last night, it was very unfortunate. Lisa tends to go over the top when there's a problem. I suppose it's only natural in the circumstances.'

'What circumstances?' Fran snapped. 'That she's got you wrapped around her little finger?'

Ivo flinched visibly.

'That isn't the sort of unsympathetic comment I would have expected from you,

Fran.'

'Of course I know Lisa's life is difficult, but you won't be here much longer. So what will she do then? Wouldn't it be better if she found local people to help out in emergencies?'

Nodding, he admitted, 'I suppose you're right. I'll talk to her about it when things have cooled down a little.'

'Perhaps it would be better coming from Gran.'

'No, not after that scene this morning.' Then he added with a rueful smile, 'I didn't know Elizabeth could get so heated.'

'We all have a dark side that we generally keep hidden,' Fran replied.

'And what's your dark side?' Ivo asked, looking at her intently as though the answer would be plainly visible on her face.

'I've loads of faults, as you know, for you accused me of one a minute ago. Unsympathetic, remember?'

Bending to pull out a weed, Ivo was obviously embarrassed.

'Sorry about that. I said it in the heat of the moment.'

'Defending Lisa,' Fran threw in.

'Perhaps. If I'm honest though, I was trying to get myself off the hook. Look, Fran, I know I did the wrong thing last night, but Lisa was in such a state. She seemed to think the blocked drain had spread all sorts of diseases and of course she worries about the boys. But the more I tried to reassure her, the more she cried, and like most men, I find it hard to cope with a tearful woman.'

He paused, waiting for Fran to speak, but she could think of nothing to say that would not cause more bad feeling between them, and that she was surprised to find herself thinking was something she did not want.

'Well, then, I'd better go and make my peace with Mrs Bowen.'

Watching him make his way to the back door, Fran sighed. Although she didn't envy Lisa her widowhood, it must be pleasant to control men by bursting into tears. Perhaps she should try it herself sometimes.

Fran decided not to go into the office until she felt Lisa had had time to calm down. But later, going in with a bill that needed paying, one look at Lisa's face told Fran that she was still upset.

'I suppose it was your doing,' she flung at Fran. 'Even though I was worried about the drains, Ivo as good as told me that in future I had to stand on my own two feet. You've been after him ever since you came here. So much for being upset by Geoff.'

'I most certainly have not been after Ivo! But you can hardly expect me to ignore him when we work together.'

'He brings you plants!'

Fran's voice rose with incredulity.

'You mean the hyacinths and polyanthus?

He was only doing his job, putting plants about the place.'

'He didn't put any in my office.'

'Oh, for goodness' sake, don't be so silly. I expect he put the plants in the study because people come in to see me.'

Fran was totally unprepared for Lisa's sudden stormy tears, or her disjointed words.

'You think Ivo's wonderful, don't you, but did you know he's taken garden plans without asking you?'

Snatching a tissue from the box on her desk, Lisa saw Fran's frown and smiled.

'You said yourself that Elizabeth wasn't paying him enough.'

'If I were you, I'd be very careful about accusing Ivo. There'll be a perfectly logical explanation.'

'If you're so sure, go and ask him about Geoff!'

Without another word, Fran left the office, her thoughts in a turmoil. But she wasn't given time to think for Elizabeth wanted to go up to the attic stairs to see the decorating.

'Gran,' Fran said slowly as they went up the back stairs, 'have you ever looked through the boxes up here to see if there is anything of historical interest about the house or gardens?'

'You mean to put on display in the house? I'm sure there are some interesting documents but I want the public to see the house as if they were actually staying here. Glass-topped display cabinets of yellowing pages wouldn't be right.'

Reaching the top of the stairs, Elizabeth stopped to look along the freshly-decorated corridor.

'I like your choice of wallpaper, Fran. It's just right.'

'It wasn't me. Ivo chose it,' Fran said flatly.

Shifting her weight on to her good leg, Elizabeth said, 'I saw you and Ivo talking this morning in the herb garden.'

Wanting to avoid her grandmother's watchful eyes, Fran opened an attic door and looked inside.

'He was just explaining about yesterday evening.'

'Fran, do you think he's in love with Lisa? It would explain a lot.'

Although her heart missed a beat, Fran managed to reply evenly.

'From what Lisa's just told me, I don't think so, but I'm not sure how she feels about him.'

'She relies on him a lot and unless he does something to lessen this dependency, I do wonder if her feelings could in time turn to love. A marriage based on pity, on being there to pick up pieces, is destined to be unhappy. But I'm always an optimist, so I hope things will still sort themselves out.'

'What do you mean still?' Fran asked, but Elizabeth was already going back down the stairs.

'There's a letter for you,' Mrs Bowen said, when Fran went into the kitchen to wash the dust of the attics off her hands. 'It was on top of the pile the postman brought and as it's marked Personal, I thought I'd give it to you directly. Sit down and read it while I make us a nice cup of tea.'

The envelope was typed and thinking it was from the advertising agency about a loose end over her sudden departure, Fran opened it. But her expression hardened when drawing out a single sheet of note paper, she recognised Geoff's writing. As though by magic, her eyes focused on one paragraph, which was the one Geoff had intended to stun her.

What a surprise to discover in the roundabout way families have that Ivo is working in the gardens at The Court, she read. *I don't suppose he's told you we're cousins. He won't want to spoil the squeaky-clean image he's now got as an up-and-coming gardening designer. But as old habits die hard, I must look him up, and see what he's up to on the sly.*

'Fran, whatever is it?' Mrs Bowen asked. 'You've gone as white as a sheet!'

'It's from Geoff. He's having one last go at being nasty.'

'Then the one place for that letter is in the rubbish bin,' Mrs Bowen declared. 'Leave unpleasant letters lying about and they fester like sores.'

Muttering something about the drawing-room fire, Fran hurried away.

If she had stayed just a little longer in the kitchen, she would have come face to face with the subject of Geoff's mischievous letter. She needed time to think, to try to calm the whirlpool of thoughts which Geoff's letter had created. The fact that Ivo hadn't told her that he and Geoff were cousins was soon cleared up, for he wouldn't want to be linked with someone who had caused so much pain. But what exactly did Geoff mean by sly? Could it be something to do with the garden plans?

CHAPTER FOURTEEN

'He's told you we're related, hasn't he?' Fran heard Ivo say as he stood watching her from the drawing-room doorway.

Fran stayed on her knees watching the shred of Geoff's letter blacken into oblivion.

'I should have told you.'

The anger in Ivo's voice was directed to himself.

'Yes, you should!' she hurled at him angrily, scrambling to her feet.

'Look, I can explain. I don't know exactly what he's said to you, but knowing him, I guess it wasn't anything to my good.'

'He told me the truth, which is more than

118

you did,' she accused. 'And you had plenty of opportunity.'

With a nod of acceptance at this, Ivo came farther into the room, but not so close as to intimidate her.

'Fran, listen to me a minute, will you? With hindsight, it would have been better coming from me, but I feared that what would happen just has.'

Then taking a deep breath as though this would help him put his side of the story more clearly, Ivo continued.

'I thought if I told you Geoff and I were cousins, you would see me as a constant reminder of him, or not give me a chance to show we are as different as chalk and cheese.'

'Yes, you would have been a reminder at first,' Fran conceded. 'I can see that. And do you know, even from the start, I felt I knew you vaguely. Your eyes are very like Geoff's and there's something in the way you walk.'

'And kissed you? Did he kiss you like I did?'

There was an underlying urgency in his question and realising what it was about, Fran replied softly, 'No, you don't kiss me like he did.'

'Fran, you just used the present tense. Does that mean . . .'

But she stopped him with a question that although quietly spoken was important.

'What about Lisa?'

'I've never kissed Lisa.'

'You seem very close, you're always up there.'

'Fran, I do believe you're jealous!'

Ivo tried to tease, but she wasn't having it. His teasing tone reminded her unpleasantly of Geoff.

'Jealous? Why should it matter to me what you get up to with Lisa?' she snapped.

'I guess that's what you said to Geoff.' Ivo was serious again. 'But I'm not him, can't you see that?' he implored. 'And as for Lisa, she's just someone who needs help. Surely you can see that?'

He paused, then seeing Fran's slight nod he continued.

'Call me stupid but it never crossed my mind that helping her would lead to anything else.'

'How about Lisa though? She's been very eager to tell me every time you've been to her house.'

Fran forced herself to look at him, watching intently for any sign that he was being evasive, just like his cousin. But all she saw was a frowning puzzlement which seemed genuine.

'In all honesty, I've never seen any indication that Lisa's taken my helping to be anything more than just that. But I can hardly go and ask her, can I? Perhaps though, it would be a good idea if when she next asks me to her house, I make some excuse.'

'What about those cosy Sunday dinners?'

Fran asked.

'They're hardly cosy with two boys there and anyway, I don't go all that often. Fran, you do believe me, don't you?'

Before she could reply, they heard footsteps hurrying away. Instinctively, they both knew it couldn't be Elizabeth, or heavy-footed Mrs Bowen, It had to be Lisa. But how much had she overheard? As Ivo turned to hurry after her, Fran put her hand on his arm.

'I'll go. It will seem more natural, for I guess she was looking for me.'

But she went slowly and reluctantly to the office. What on earth was she going to say to Lisa? Ask her point blank if she had overheard anything? No, that wouldn't do for it was as good as accusing her of deliberately listening. Standing outside the office door she held her breath the better to hear if there was the faintest muffled sob, but there was silence.

The speed with which she opened the door surprised Lisa.

'Fran, you gave me a fright bursting in like that. Is anything the matter?'

In the short time it had taken Lisa to speak, Fran had searched her face, alert for any sign of being upset, but she could see none.

'No, there's nothing wrong.'

She paused, then deciding honesty was best, she continued.

'Ivo and I were talking in the drawing-room and as I left, I thought I saw you disappearing.

121

Did you want me?'

'Oh, you know it's nice to have a chat sometimes. The boys, well, they're too young and Mrs Bowen loves to gossip which I don't much care for.'

'And she's got big ears at times!' Fran added lightly. Then, 'Look, shall we go into the garden? I can't see Mrs Bowen sneaking from bush to bush.'

To avoid the housekeeper, they left by the front door and as they passed the drawing-room, Fran was relieved to see Ivo had left. Once on the gravel drive, they both hesitated for the same reason, though neither realised it. They didn't want to come face to face with Ivo.

'Let's walk down the drive,' Fran suggested. 'We'll have more privacy there.'

As they scrunched along the gravel, they both looked straight ahead, Lisa wondering how to start, Fran's heart beating rapidly at the thought that Lisa might be going to say that Ivo mattered a lot to her. It was Lisa who began slowly.

'Ivo and Elizabeth have both been very good to me . . .'

When she paused, Fran nodded encouragingly. She wanted this conversation to be over, and quickly.

'I've found it very hard after Alan.'

Lisa so obviously didn't want to say any more and Fran quickly put a comforting hand on her arm. Much to her surprise, Lisa took hold of it. Was it, Fran wondered, for comfort, or to prepare her for something unpleasant.

'I'm leaving here!'

Lisa spoke so rapidly that it took a few seconds for Fran to realise what she had said.

'Leaving?' she repeated. 'But why? Is there a problem?'

'Of sorts. It's Ivo.'

Fran stopped, steeling herself. Was Lisa going to tell her something which would expose Ivo as a liar? That they had been having an affair? And what did Lisa know about the slyness that Geoff had hinted about?

But Lisa was speaking again.

'Isn't it strange how relationships have a habit of going the way you don't want them to go?'

Lisa stopped, seeming preoccupied with drawing a wavy line with the toe of her shoe in the loose gravel. Now Fran was quite certain what was coming next. Lisa was leaving, going to London to prepare for the wedding.

'The boys are getting too used to Ivo being about the place. Since Alan, he's been wonderful with them.'

Frowning, Fran shook her head slightly as though to get her scrambled thoughts into some sort of order. Was Lisa saying she didn't want her sons to become too attached to Ivo? Glancing up and seeing Fran's puzzlement, Lisa smiled.

'I was never much good at being concise,

orderly. Perhaps that's why I've let things drift with Ivo. You see, Fran, I don't want Ivo to think he's got to marry me because the boys need a father.'

'Has he proposed then?' Fran forced out.

'Good gracious, no! I don't think it's even crossed his mind, yet. But as time goes by, we might find ourselves being propelled along by the need of the boys for a father.'

'So you don't love Ivo?' Fran tried to sound casual.

Lisa sighed regretfully.

'It might be a lot easier if I did. But anyway, Ivo doesn't love me. He's kind and thoughtful and I've come to rely on him too much. So you see, I've got to go. I want to make a clean break and that wouldn't be possible with Ivo coming back occasionally to check the garden. Don't worry, I'm not going to Bristol to some awful flat! Alan's uncle has a large farm and a few weeks ago offered me a cottage in return for help with his accounts.'

'Oh, I'm so glad!' Fran exclaimed, then wondering if she had sounded too delighted, she asked hurriedly, 'But why did you rush away from the drawing-room?'

'I could hardly have said all I have to you, in front of Ivo. It would have been very awkward because well, you know men, they're not very perceptive and he would have not the slightest idea that we might be drifting into . . . well, you know,' she added again.

If Lisa was surprised at the strength of Fran's quick hug she did not show it and neither did Fran show her relief that now things were a little clearer between herself and Ivo.

'So will you tell Elizabeth?' Lisa asked as they began to retrace their steps. 'That's what I was coming to ask you, but when I heard Ivo was with you, well, I suppose I took fright and ran!'

'Why come to me first? Gran is very understanding.'

'And that's exactly why I didn't want to tell her I was leaving! I felt she would soon have me telling her all about Ivo and I didn't want that. Fran, don't get me wrong, but Elizabeth can be a bit of an organiser, and I didn't want her trying to sort things out about Ivo. It would have been awful had she told him I was worrying that he might ask me to marry him out of pity.'

Fran nodded in sympathy. Yes, to put it kindly, Elizabeth could be over helpful at times. Although Lisa had gone with a lighter heart back into the house, Fran knew she would be unable to work until she had thought about all the implications of Lisa's news. So not wanting to bump into Elizabeth until things were clearer in her mind, she decided to find a secluded bench in the garden.

She walked quickly to the wildlife pool on the edge of the woodland. Sweeping dead leaves and twigs off the bench, she smiled as she sat down. When she was a child, she had often come to the pool to look for tadpoles, frogs and other water creatures. Little had she thought then that as an adult she would be sitting there trying to sort out her tangled emotions.

Although she seemed to be looking at the pool, her eyes were unfocused, unseeing. Astonished at the strength of her relief about Lisa's reasons for leaving, she tried hard to push away the fact that Ivo was very much part of this. Ivo . . . a wave of sadness and regret had her sighing.

If only he wasn't Geoff's cousin, things might have been so very different. She thought she had broken free of Geoff, but still he was influencing her life. It wasn't fair!

So to be in charge of her own destiny, she determined to look at everything dispassionately. First she must try to sort out her feelings about Ivo. Without realising she was doing so, she began to count out her thoughts on her fingers. Did she like him? Yes. But was she in love with him? She hesitated as scenes flashed by of her with Ivo, in the herb garden, the pots of flowers he had brought, his kisses, few though they had been.

Then a sudden dark thought shouldered all of this away. What about the mystery of Ivo searching in the attic and library? What exactly was he doing with what looked like old garden

126

plans of The Court? Black despair made her shiver and, getting up, she rubbed her arms as she walked around the pool. Having been blind to Geoff's faults, she did not want to make the same painful mistake again. But Ivo wasn't Geoff! Apart from those garden plans, everything about him was decent, honest, open, so there had to be an innocent explanation, there just had to be!

The sound of a lawn mower reminding Fran that she could not stand there all day, there was work to do, she hurried back to the house.

It was over lunch in the little dining-room that Fran told her grandmother Lisa was leaving. She had prepared herself for some searching questions but to her surprise, Elizabeth just commented it was for the best. But she did ask if Lisa had given any indication of when this might be. Thinking her grandmother might be worrying about the office work, Fran hurriedly reassured her that she would take over Lisa's work for as long as was needed.

'I'm glad for Ivo,' Elizabeth seemed to be saying it to herself, but Fran was quick to ask why. 'I've been worried he might find himself sliding helplessly into a marriage with Lisa.'

This was so near what Lisa had been saying just a few hours before that Fran could not hide her surprise which Elizabeth was quick to see.

'I suppose you didn't see it as a possibility

because, having decided Geoff and Ivo were carbon copies, you never thought any good of Ivo, only bad.'

Fran did not even try to deny this, for she knew this to be true. Hurriedly finishing her lunch, she left with the excuse that she had a lot to do. But having shut the dining-room door behind her, she hesitated, the urge to see Ivo growing with every passing minute. She did not look for a reason for this, beyond letting him know of Lisa's plans.

She found him in one of the greenhouses, tending the pot plants which would be needed in the house.

'Ivo, have you a minute?' she asked tentatively, opening the door.

With a welcoming smile, he motioned she should close the door.

'Sorry, I forgot,' she said, then falling silent she picked up a dark-red African violet and examined it closely. Now she was with him; she didn't quite know how to bring up the subject of Lisa.

'Are you inspecting that for any signs of disease?' he asked mildly.

Hastily replacing the pot, her words ran together in her anxious haste.

'Lisa is leaving, going to an uncle. There's a cottage and work and the boys will have their uncle.'

'That's great news!'

She was so taken aback by his swift reply

that she looked up at him for the first time since coming into the greenhouse.

'You seem surprised,' he said. 'Fran, why don't you sit down? This high stool is clean.'

'I've work to do,' she began, but he silenced her by gently placing his hands on her shoulders to encourage her to sit.

He remained standing, leaning against the wooden staging, arms folded.

'Fran, I want you to know that despite what it looked like at times, I have never felt anything for Lisa and her boys, other than concern. It's very important to me that you believe it.'

He paused then seeing her nod, he continued.

'There seemed to me to be two major obstacles between us, Geoff and Lisa.'

'I've told you, Geoff is in the past, and I want you to believe that! I'm just sorry I let my hurt over him colour my . . . my . . .'

She trailed off, not knowing how to finish, bending her head so he wouldn't see her confusion.

'Opinion of me?' he suggested. 'And what about now, when I'm no longer in Geoff's shadow?'

Although he was waiting, she didn't reply, not because the words weren't there, but because she was frightened by the enormity of them. After Geoff, she had built a high protective wall around her, but now it was tumbling down as though shaken by an earthquake.

'Sorry, I shouldn't have asked that.'

Pushing himself away from the staging, he turned to reach for a cyclamen.

'Now, it's me who's sorry. It's just that I'm finding it difficult to find the right words.'

Putting the plant down, he took her hand, standing directly in front of her, so close that she had to bend her head back to look up at him. They said nothing, both of them overwhelmed by the nearness of the other. But something in Fran's eyes gave Ivo the courage to take a step along the path he had been wanting to follow ever since the first time he had seen her.

'Fran, I want to get to know you better.'

'Me, too!' she added quickly. Then flustered, she explained, 'I mean I'd like to know you better, too!'

'Good, that's a beginning.'

He smiled, trying not to look at her very tempting mouth.

'Ivo, I want you to know I trust you,' she said thinking of the garden plans.

There had to be a simple reason for him taking them. He wasn't in the least like Geoff.

'I would never do, or say, anything to hurt you.'

As though controlled by a force he was incapable of resisting, Ivo bent to kiss her. She did not hesitate to return his kiss, her arms

130

going around his neck to pull him closer. It was the sound of clapping that forced them apart, Fran red-faced with embarrassment, Ivo giving the two gardeners a look which made them beat a hasty retreat.

'I suppose people in glasshouses should be careful what they do,' Ivo said ruefully.

'There are plenty of better places in the grounds I could show you,' Fran offered, eyes dancing.

'Not now though.' Ivo laughed. Then suddenly serious he asked, 'There'll be plenty of time for that later, won't there?'

'All the time in the world,' she whispered.

'Fran,' he warned, 'Elizabeth is coming towards us.'

'What on earth can she want!' Fran muttered. 'What is it that's bringing everyone here?'

'In Elizabeth's case, I think I know. I've had some old papers about the garden bound as a surprise for her. The book should have come today and had the parcel addressed to her.'

'Well, my dears!'

Elizabeth greeted them a little out of breath from hurrying, clutching the bound book tightly to her. Then looking intently at Fran and Ivo, she smiled.

'It isn't only the garden designs that have worked out just as I wanted,' she said as she lovingly watched the two people who were so dear to her.